The
Beautiful
and the
Damned

The Beautiful
and the
Damned

Jessica Verday

SIMON PULSE

NEW YORK LONDON TORONTO SYDNEY NEW DELHI

SIMON PULSE

An imprint of Simon & Schuster Children's Publishing Division
1230 Avenue of the Americas, New York, NY 10020
First Simon Pulse hardcover edition October 2013
Copyright © 2013 by Jessica Verday
All rights reserved, including the right of reproduction in whole or in part in any form.
SIMON PULSE and colophon are registered trademarks of Simon & Schuster, Inc.
For information about special discounts for bulk purchases,
please contact Simon & Schuster Special Sales at 1-866-506-1949
or business@simonandschuster.com.
The Simon & Schuster Speakers Bureau can bring authors to your live event.
For more information or to book an event contact
the Simon & Schuster Speakers Bureau at 1-866-248-3049
or visit our website at www.simonspeakers.com.
Jacket designed by Regina Flath
Interior designed by Paul Weil and Karina Granda
The text of this book was set in Caslon.
Manufactured in the United States of America
2 4 6 8 10 9 7 5 3 1
Library of Congress Cataloging-in-Publication Data
Verday, Jessica.
The beautiful and the damned / Jessica Verday.
p. cm.
Summary: Cyn, a witch, and Avian, executioner of the truly evil, discover that
Cyn is an Echo, a conduit for souls of the dead, who will lose control unless she risks
her life to vanquish the source of her power in Sleepy Hollow.
ISBN 978-1-4424-8835-9 (hc)
[1. Supernatural—Fiction. 2. Memory—Fiction. 3. Demonology—Fiction.
4. Angels—Fiction. 5. Vampires—Fiction. 6. Dead—Fiction.] I. Title.
PZ7.V5828Be 2013
[Fic]—dc23
2013016758
ISBN 978-1-4424-8839-7 (eBook)

For Lee, who knows how to fix it when I break it

ACKNOWLEDGMENTS

Special thanks to my Foundry team for working with me on this project: Mollie Glick, for being so dedicated and taking it (literally) down to the wire—you are a super agent; Katie Hamblin, for taking such good care of me; Rachel Hecht for keeping track of the million and one foreign details; and Deirdre Smerillo and Melissa Moorehead for their tireless contract work.

Special thanks to Liesa Abrams and Simon Pulse for jumping in and loving this Cynical little book, and to Michael Strother for finding the answers when I need them!

Special thanks to F. Scott Fitzgerald for the use of the title. And a special thanks to my readers—without you this book wouldn't exist. Thank you for your time and your trust in me.

PREFACE

Show me a hero and I'll write you a tragedy.

—F. Scott Fitzgerald

Sleepy Hollow, NY
August

Y ou *will* give me the keys."

Cyn Hargrave's eyes opened wide. She didn't know it, but her pupils were dilating. Black swallowing green irises. The man in front of her was defenseless.

"Sure."

He handed over a small plastic key fob. The sappy, love-struck grin on his face disgusted her.

"Stop staring at me like that," she ordered. Anxiously looking over her shoulder again, Cyn could almost hear the police sirens that she knew would be coming.

The besotted man just sighed happily. Like he didn't care what she was doing.

"Yeah—okay, then." She grabbed the key ring and turned toward the silver sports car sitting two inches away from the nearby curb.

Stop. Forgetting something.

She turned back to the man, pupils flaring again. "You, sit. Wait. And don't think about me while I'm gone."

"Okay," the man said, and promptly sat down.

Cyn returned to the car, wishing as she threw open the door that she had more time to admire the black racing stripe curving sexily up the hood. A red-leather interior screamed her name, and she answered its siren call, sliding behind the steering wheel.

With a flick of her wrist, the engine roared to life, and for just an instant she closed her eyes, savoring the feel. *Finally.* Something she was in control of.

But the sweet rush didn't last long. It was chased away again by the pounding urge to check her rearview mirror for those flashing red and blue lights.

They have to know what I did by now. There was so much blood. . . .

A streak of crimson still stained the back of her right pinky. She'd scrubbed for twenty minutes to get it all off, but it wasn't enough. She wondered if Hunter's blood would always be on her hands.

Flinching at the sight, Cyn quickly rubbed her hand against her leg as she peeled out, pushing the car into third gear and then fourth as soon as she hit the highway.

Three states away, she finally allowed herself to breathe.

Chapter One

Hampton Falls, NH
Two months later

The wig was cheap. It made her head itch. A synthetic material, poorly made. Cyn had found it in the donations bin of a Goodwill thrift store. Probably somebody's Saturday-night castoff. But it made her feel better to have it on. Protected.

"Brunette tonight, huh?" One of the cooks leaned over the disposal in the sink, trying to fish something out of it. "Thought blondes have more fun."

"They do, Lenny." Cyn opened another button on the top of her waitress uniform. "Get better tips, too. Guess I'll just have to use my other charms."

"Don't forget who takes care of you around here."

Tucking her pad into her waist pocket, Cyn blew him a kiss before heading to the counter. "I don't know what you're talking about."

"Yeah, yeah. Just remember when you bring back all that green that *I'm* the guy who does the dishes for you at the end of your shift." Cyn waved two fingers dismissively, like she couldn't hear what he was saying. "*And* snaked your ring from the drain last week when you dropped it!" he shouted after her.

Cyn glanced down at the knotted gold ring on her right hand, rubbing it with her thumb. But she didn't respond.

"Don't know how that girl does it," Lenny muttered to himself. "I swear she bewitches those customers or something." He plunged his hand one last time into the sink and pulled out a bent spoon before adding it to the pile in the box by the back door.

"Order up," Marv called from the kitchen pass-through. He sat a plate full of steamed clams on the counter and moved to the next ticket, wiping a greasy hand on his once-white apron.

Cyn deliberately ignored him, returning an empty coffeepot to the coffeemaker. The diner was half-full, but she liked to take her time.

"Yo, Cynsation." Marv rapped on a dented silver bell. "I said, *order up*."

"Calm down, Marv. I heard you." She rolled her eyes and grabbed the plate. "It's under the warmer. It'll be fine."

Dropping the food at table nine, Cyn noticed the empty mug in front of a burly man sitting on a bar stool at the counter. "Do you need a fill-up?" she stopped to ask.

He paused, half-eaten ham sandwich dripping mayo and bits of lettuce down his shirt. "If you're doing the filling, sweetheart, then I'm doing the taking. But we could rearrange those positions if you'd be so inclined. My truck's parked right outside." He flashed a smile of rotted teeth and half-chewed food particles at her.

Cyn leaned in, making sure that the barely buttoned uniform she wore gaped in the front. "*Inclined?* I do love a man who uses big words."

The trucker ogled her hopefully. "You do? 'Cuz I know a million of 'em."

"Well, I just want you to remember one little word. . . ." Eyes wide, pupils flaring, she said, "*Tip.*"

As soon as the trucker was gone Cyn pocketed his seventy-five percent tip and scanned the dining room, judging the beverage-fulfillment needs of her customers. Table three was a guzzler: he'd already gone through two refills before his meal had even arrived. But tables four and five were moving at a slower pace.

Marv lifted a hand to ring the bell again, and she fixed him with a steely glare. Throwing both hands up in the air, he slowly backed off and retreated to the kitchen.

But before Cyn could grab the order that was waiting, a blast of chilly air hit her from behind. October in New Hampshire was cold—colder than the idiot who was currently holding the door open for longer than was necessary must have realized.

She turned to watch him come in. Stamping his feet and blowing on his hands, he looked like a glossy-magazine-styled, twenty-something wannabe hipster. Dark hair artfully tousled, with a gray scarf draped carefully around the top of a fitted jacket.

Cyn dismissed him without a second thought.

The door blasted open again, and this time a teenager came in. Young, blond, and full of spoiled-brat swagger. Cyn recognized *him* right away. Stephen Grant. All hands and no manners. He thought his daddy's money could buy him whatever, and whoever, he wanted.

She didn't like the attitude, but she *loved* making him spend some of that money on her.

Turning back to the still-steaming plate, she checked the

ticket and then dropped the food off at table four. The hipster took table seven. Right next to the back exit.

Stephen sauntered up to the counter and made a show of flipping through the menu even though it was plain to see that what he really wanted wasn't on it. He cast a calculating look at Cyn, then motioned her over. "When are you going to let me sweep you out of here?"

"Are you insinuating that I'm in need of rescuing?" Cyn flipped over her pad to a fresh sheet and clicked the end of her pen open.

"Yeah. And I can be your Prince Charming. Like the fairy tale."

"Baby, if this was a fairy tale, I'd be more interested in marrying your father and becoming a queen instead of playing princess to a punk like you." She leaned in and whispered, "He's the one with all the money, after all. . . ."

It probably wasn't the smartest thing to say, but he just pissed her off in all the wrong ways. With his slick arrogance and give-me-what-I-want attitude.

Flushed red with anger, Stephen slammed the menu down. "I want a tuna on rye with a side of pickles," he said coldly.

"Coming right up."

"Bitch."

She could feel his gaze burning through her back as she walked away. Mentally sighing, Cyn reached up to straighten the back of her wig and kept moving to table seven. "What can I get for you?" she asked, all bright smiles and eager eyes.

The customers never had any idea just how much of an act it all was.

"Coffee. Black," Hipster said.

"You got it."

She told Marv about the tuna ticket, and by the time she'd filled Hipster's coffee, her order was ready. As she picked up Stephen's plate, Cyn wished she had opened another button. Sometimes that was easier than dealing with him.

Sliding the plate onto the table, she said, "Enjoy your meal." She was turning to walk away when his voice stopped her.

"I asked for my bread to be lightly toasted."

"No, you didn't."

"Well, that's the way I want it."

Cyn gave him an irritated look. "Why don't you just eat your food the way it is and stop bothering me? That's not too much to ask, now, is it?"

He seemed to think about it for a moment. Then he said, "Yes. It is."

"Excuse me?"

"I want my sandwich remade, and this time it should be *lightly toasted*."

Cyn reached for the plate. "Sure," she said through gritted teeth. "I'll get that fixed right up for you."

Marv was in the middle of slopping dirty water onto the floor and pushing it around with a wet mop when Cyn entered the kitchen. He eyed up what she had in her hands and shook his head. "Nope. Sorry. I can't remake anything. Cleaning duty."

"S'okay, Marv. I got it." Scraping the plate clean into the trash, Cyn grabbed a new one from the stack on the prep counter. Then she put two pieces of bread into the toaster and went to the fridge to get a fresh pack of tuna, some mayonnaise and relish, and the jar of sliced pickles. When the toaster popped, Cyn carefully inspected the bread to make sure it was *lightly toasted* before putting it all together. New sandwich in hand, she walked out of the kitchen to deliver it to her customer.

The guzzler at table three was frantically trying to wave her down again as she passed, but she just smiled at him and held up one finger. He could wait another minute or two. It wasn't like her tip would suffer for it.

"Here you go." Cyn plunked the plate down in front of

Stephen. "One freshly made tuna on rye, *lightly toasted*, with pickles on the side."

He looked up from his phone, feigning surprise at her arrival, and inspected the sandwich. Cyn waited for him to deem it good enough, but he didn't say a word.

Until she walked away again.

"Um, miss?"

Oh, he's going to leave me a huge *tip for this.*

Cyn pivoted back around to face him. "What is it now?"

"I've decided I don't want the pickles."

"That's what you have a napkin for. Use it."

His face cracked a little bit. That smooth, fake smile dissolved into a sneer. "I don't want them sitting on the napkin *next* to me. I don't want them sitting anywhere *near* me."

This was moving beyond big-tip territory into straight-up petition-for-sainthood territory.

"Fine." Cyn picked up one of the pickles. In two crunches, it was gone. She picked up the second one and devoured it just as quickly. Taking a moment to lick her lips, she ran her tongue over her teeth and smiled widely. "Problem solved."

Stephen looked down at his plate and then back to her. "What about the juice?"

Reaching down, she slowly ran her finger over the left-behind pickle juice and brought it to her lips. He watched her with wide eyes, never taking them off her mouth as she sucked her finger clean.

Cyn *knew* she shouldn't be baiting him like this—it was only going to give him the wrong idea.

And she was right.

With one smooth motion, Stephen gripped her wrist. Jerking her toward him.

Cyn had to consciously unclench her teeth to spit out the words "Let go of me. *Now.*"

Stephen let go all right. But only because the hipster from table seven was suddenly there, introducing Stephen's face to the counter.

"Be nice," Hipster said.

Stephen made a choking noise as his fingers fell away from Cyn's wrist. "What the fuck, man? Let me up."

All eyes in the diner were on them now. Even with her ever-rotating assortment of wigs, Cyn tried to stick to normal hair colors and bland clothes. The idea was *not* to get noticed. *So much for not making a scene.*

"Thanks," Cyn said quietly as the guy let up on Stephen's face. "Just a misunderstanding."

Stephen stood up and kicked the nearest stool out of his

way. "I'm *not* paying for that," he sneered, gesturing to the plate. "And *you* can expect a call from my dad's lawyer. Maybe even the cops," he said to the hipster.

Cyn froze when she saw him size Stephen up and then reach inside his jacket, exposing the gun that was tucked into a side holster there.

"No need." He pulled out a badge and flashed it. "Officer Declan Thomas. I'm with the Sleepy Hollow Police Department."

CHAPTER TWO

Avian Alexander pushed his motorcycle up to the entrance of Pete's Salvage Yard and put the kickstand down, taking in the heavily padlocked gates that stood before him. The radiator hose on his bike had been patched one time too many, and today was the day it gave up the ghost.

The day the damned junkyard was closed.

He was considering breaking in when his cell phone rang. "Father Montgomery?"

"Ah, I'm glad I could reach you."

Avian smiled. "Finally decided to get a cell phone and join the—what century are we in now?"

"Twenty-first. And no, I fear I have not fully embraced

technology yet. I'm using the phone at the rectory. Are you on your way home?"

"I'm going to be later than expected. A part blew on my bike."

"Are you all right?" Father Montgomery asked. Then he chuckled. "What am I thinking? Of course you are. But this bike of yours, it's older than I am. When are you going to replace it?"

Avian glanced down at the motorcycle. It would have been a hell of a lot easier to just go and buy a brand-new Harley. It wasn't like he couldn't afford to. He just didn't want to.

"You know I like my toys old and with a little dirt on them. Like me."

"My boy, you may be indestructible, but the humans sharing the road with you aren't." The years of familiarity that spanned between them was evident in the gentle chiding.

Father Montgomery was the *only* one who got away with that.

"You worry too much."

"You're probably right. But just the same, I'll leave the outside light on for you. Let me know when you get in."

"I will."

"Hey, we're closed," a man on the other side of the gates called. "You'll have to come back tomorrow."

Avian pocketed his phone and looked up. The man's blue

work shirt had the name PETE embroidered on it. Before Avian could respond, Pete's eyes opened wide. "Holy shit. Is that a Vincent Black Lightning? I've never seen one in person before."

"Vintage 1948. Only thirty were ever made." Avian leaned against the bike and crossed his arms. "So, what was that you said about being closed?"

Pete unlocked the gate. "Nothin'. We're open now."

As Avian checked the new radiator hose he and Pete had just put on, something from the far side of the junkyard caught his attention. Something he hadn't seen in a long time. He put two fingers to his mouth and whistled. The large black animal came straight to him.

"Nice dog," Avian said.

Pete's face grew nervous.

Anyone else looking at the beast would see something that resembled a cross between a rottweiler and a pit bull. Broad shoulders, massive paws, and oddly colored eyes. There was nothing on the surface to reveal its true nature. But Avian saw what was behind the veil.

Steam rising from its fur. The scent of sulfur on its breath. And eyes that burned hellfire. One bite from this animal, and you would not be long for this world.

Pete's Salvage Yard was being guarded by a hellhound.

"Is this land consecrated?" Avian asked. Hellhounds only protected sacred ground.

Pete glanced around and then nodded. "Used to be an old German church back in the fifties. Sat right over there." He pointed off to the left. "The congregation grew old, and they all passed on. Their heirs sold it to my pops, and he bulldozed everything. With their permission, of course." Pete crossed himself, and Avian fought back an automatic response to recoil at the gesture. "The graveyard is on the other side of the lot. I don't put any cars over there unless it gets really full and I have to."

The hellhound came closer and pushed his head into Avian's outstretched hand, causing dark curls of steam to weave through his fingers. Wrapping around them like smoke-laden tattoos. The scars on Avian's back burned in response, and the dog whined.

"I know, boy," he said softly. "Sometimes I miss it too."

Pete looked on in awe. "He *never* lets anyone touch him. I just inherited him along with the junkyard when my pops died. Doesn't even have a name."

Avian gestured for the dog to return to his post. Slinging one leg over his bike, he started the engine. "I can relate. Every-one I know just calls me Thirteen."

CHAPTER THREE

Cyn tried to ignore the cop after he escorted Stephen to the door and then went back to his table and his coffee. But every minute felt like it stretched into an eternity of waiting. Waiting for him to say the words that began with "You're under arrest" and ended with her being hauled off to jail.

She tried to play it cool as she cleared away dishes and refilled drinks. Resisted every screaming impulse inside her brain that told her to steal the closest car and run away as fast as she could. But then she noticed the cigarette. It was resting on an overturned jelly holder.

Figures. Just when she was trying to quit.

Face carefully blank, Cyn grabbed the coffeepot and carried it over to him. "More coffee?" Then she said, "You can't smoke in here."

Declan glanced over at the cigarette casually. "I'm not smoking it."

"You can't have it lit, either."

"Right." He picked it up and ground it into the jelly container. "I'll have some more coffee, then."

Cyn smiled at him as she poured. "That was really nice of you to help me out with Stephen. But where's your uniform?" One hand went to her hip. Straining the buttons across her top that weren't already open.

"I'm off duty," he replied. "Just up here for a little R & R."

She'd already turned to take the coffeepot back when his voice stopped her. "Any recommendations?"

"Hmmm?" Cyn played dumb long enough to buy her some time to think about the places she'd heard some of the locals mention. *Downtown. The harbor. Tom's Crab Shack. Just say any one of those.*

"Any recommendations for what I should do. Things to see? You're a native . . . aren't you?"

"You should try Tom's Crab Shack. But go on a Wednesday night. That's when they offer the all-you-can-eat special. Biggest crabs around." Her hands were getting sweaty, the coffeepot was slipping. "Here's your check."

Cyn placed the check facedown on the table and then retreated to the kitchen. The silver bell dinged for her attention again, and by the time she delivered her last order of the night, the cop was gone. It took every ounce of self-control she had to walk calmly over to his table.

I bet he didn't even leave me a tip.

But when she reached for his check, she saw the $1.24 he owed for the coffee . . . right on top of a crisp fifty-dollar bill. Then she saw what else he'd left behind too.

His card, with the words CALL ME written on it.

The sky was inky black with a haze of gray around the edges when Cyn started walking home from the diner. Marv had said he'd only need her for a couple of hours tonight, and for once, he'd been right.

Sunrise was a long way off, though, and Cyn didn't like to sleep at night. The dark brought bad things. Nightmares, with claws. And teeth. She liked to sleep during the day, in the brightest puddle of sunshine she could find.

Two blocks away from her apartment, Cyn took a shortcut through an alley. Passing by an old brick hotel, she stuffed her hands into her pockets and walked faster. When the back of her neck suddenly tingled, she spun around. A second later the windows ten stories up exploded as two men fell from the building, locked in a spiraling death grip.

Giant shards of glass preceded the falling shadows and shattered into a million pieces when they hit the ground. Less than a foot away from it all, Cyn took cover behind a stack of empty boxes sitting next to a Dumpster and covered her face with her hands, waiting for the cacophony to end.

But it was only just beginning.

They landed with a sickening crunch. Flesh and bone meeting hard pavement and freshly ground glass. The fall should have killed them. But they only seemed momentarily stunned before getting to their feet. Cyn peeked out from beneath her wig, which was hanging lopsided and obscuring one eye.

Both of the men were dressed in dark clothes, but one was much larger than the other. He stood a full head taller as they sized each other up. That didn't stop the smaller man, though, who bared his teeth and charged straight at his opponent, latching onto his throat. The sound the bigger man made as he tried to get away echoed bitter agony inside Cyn's head.

In the dark, they passed for two brawling humans. But

when their faces turned to the light, Cyn could see they were something else entirely. The small man had a bull-shaped face and long black horns that curled down beneath his chin. The bigger man had a dog's head, a short snout, and droopy ears.

The dog-faced man suddenly twisted to one side, coming dangerously close to where Cyn was hiding. She cupped her hands over her mouth to quiet her breathing. He pulled free, blood dripping from a gash in his neck, and wiped a hand across his throat. Wheezing from the damage to his esophagus, he shook his head once and then launched himself at the smaller man full force.

When they collided, they slammed into the building next to the hotel and went down. A tsunami of dirt and bricks rained upon them, leaving gaping black holes in the foundation and jagged cracks that ran up the walls.

Stay calm. Don't draw attention to yourself. It's almost over.

Cyn would have thought she was going crazy if she hadn't seen glimpses of strange things her entire life. Shadows that moved. The feeling that someone was always following her. The faces living beneath hers. . . .

And then there was that night at the bridge in Sleepy Hollow, with its weird jumble of mixed-up memories of a girl named Abbey who was alive and going to high school with her one moment, then dead and buried for months the next. It was almost like *both* things had happened at once.

Ever since that night, things hadn't been the same.

Suddenly, the smaller man got the upper hand again, pinning the larger man on his back. Cyn knew what was coming next and closed her eyes so she wouldn't have to see it. Because of this, she didn't react in time when the dog-headed man reached for something to throw at his attacker, and a brick went sailing past the boxes she was hiding behind.

She only registered the sharp pain against the back of her head for a brief moment before everything went dark.

She lost half an hour lying in that dirty alley, and when she came to, both of the men were gone. The only signs that either of them had been there were the piles of bricks and broken glass still littering the ground, and a greenish puddle of goo that Cyn didn't want to stare too long at.

She didn't know what had happened, but at least there wasn't blood on her hands this time.

Stumbling, head spinning, she made it back to her apartment. The two blocks felt more like two miles, but somehow she made it.

Of course, her "apartment" was just the back room of an

abandoned print shop. It didn't have a kitchen, and the bathroom consisted only of a meager toilet stall and dirty sink. But her plants had lots of sunlight, and no one came around. All she had to worry about was keeping the mice away.

Cyn's head ached as she entered the building. A lump the size of a tennis ball had formed at the base of her neck, and it was sore to the touch. Darkness cloaked the corners of the room, and she was so exhausted she barely remembered to tug the string attached to the dim overhead lightbulb as she headed to her sleeping bag.

It was there the dreams found her.

Blood was everywhere. Her hands were warm with it. Wet with it. Dark and sticky, it looked like she'd rolled around in a mud puddle. It stained the sheets, and was spattered all over her clothes.

"Hunter . . ." She stared at her hands before she looked over at him. "There's something wrong with me."

But Hunter couldn't reply. Because Hunter was dead.

His eyes, wide and glassy, stared up at the ceiling above his prone body. From her position beside him, Cyn could tell even without leaning over that his heart wasn't beating. The lack of a steady rise and fall of his chest and the coloring of his face and hands confirmed it. That warm, sun-kissed skin that had always stayed so tan without him even trying was now the shade of cheap copier paper. Sallow and gray.

"Hunter!" She screamed his name, and this, this was her undoing.

Her hands flew to him, fingers grasping greedily at the torn edges of his chest. Trying to stuff back in the spilled intestines that hung like shiny ropes from the slit in his belly. But her hands slipped. Slid. Couldn't grab hold. Couldn't find purchase in the mass of warm, wet blood that soaked through the sheets and dripped to the floor in a steady pattern that sounded like rain.

When she said his name a second time, it was a raw moan. An anguished plea of fury and pain and heartbreak all rolled into one. "Hunter . . ."

There was fresh blood on her pillow when Cyn opened her eyes. She'd managed to scratch her cheek in her sleep. Tucking the edges of the sleeping bag beneath her chin, she sat up.

She longed for a shower, but the locker room she usually snuck into and used after her shift at the diner wasn't open until eight. A quick glance at her clock told her it was only a little after three a.m. Her wig had fallen off in her sleep and she raked cold fingers through red curls—her real hair color. The portable thrift-store heater that sat next to the sleeping bag had seen better days and only heated a small portion of the large space around her.

Scrubbing her hands across her face, Cyn got up and paced the wide expanse of concrete floor. The room was void of furniture except for a wooden chair and a three-legged table propped up by a battered copy of *The Bell Jar*. A half-open suitcase spilled forth its meager contents of clothing by the floor-to-ceiling windows that made up the entire length of the opposite wall.

A dozen plants with brown leaves and shriveled blossoms created a barricade of shrubbery in front of the windows—her guardians against all of the bad things out there.

Cyn walked over to the plants and stood before a ficus tree. Digging her fingers into the dirt, she pictured the leaves whole and healthy. In response, one of the leaves unfurled, the color changing from a brittle brown to a soft green before changing back again.

"That's it," she said. "I knew there was hope for you. You'll get there."

Warmth surged up through her fingertips from the cool earth, and she smiled. Cyn had always had a soft spot for plants, especially the half-dead ones. She liked the challenge of bringing them back to life.

Then she made the mistake of glancing up at one of the cracked windows in front of her. It wasn't her face that reflected there. It was *his*. Whoever was inside her.

Male features were superimposed over her own face. Like

a living Día de los Muertos skull. Pale skin, dark eye sockets, teeth stretched wide. His leering smile was a sucker punch, and her heart sank.

"Oh, no," Cyn said. "Not again."

CHAPTER FOUR

Avian knew that Father Montgomery was bound to be asleep by the time he parked his bike in the old shed next to the rectory. Between the radiator hose on his bike going and the Grenabli demon/vampire fight he'd interrupted in an alleyway on his way back from the salvage yard, it was almost two thirty in the morning.

He brushed some of the dead vampire's ash off his coat sleeve. "Interrupted" was the wrong word. The Grenabli demon and the vampire had tried to team up against him, but he'd single-handedly taken both of them out with the blade he kept strapped between his shoulders. The vampire's body had turned to ash. But the Grenabli's cleanup wasn't quite so easy—he was still a pile of green mush in the alley where he'd fallen.

Avian thought about going in through the back door and waiting until morning to see Father Montgomery, but he knew he wouldn't be able to quiet the nagging in his gut until he saw the old priest. Lately, something had just felt . . . off.

His heavy boots made no sound as he entered the unlocked house, and there he found Father Montgomery fast asleep in a leather armchair by the fire, the book he'd been reading still draped across his lap, the blanket he'd thrown off puddling at his feet.

With a snore and a snort, Father Montgomery woke when Avian put a hand on his shoulder. "What? Who's there?"

"It's just me, Father." Avian noticed the glasses that had slid into the chair cushion. "Your glasses are by your side."

Father Montgomery sat up and dug into the chair for them. Once they were in place, he gave Avian a beaming smile and stood to properly greet him. "Welcome home, my boy. It's so good to see you."

Avian's broad-shouldered six-foot-five-inch frame, made even bulkier by the black leather coat he was wearing, dwarfed the priest's own hunched posture, but he bent to return the hug without hesitation. "It's good to see you, too. But we need to have a talk about you leaving the door unlocked before falling asleep. Anyone could have walked in."

"That's the *point*, Avian."

Another thing only Father Montgomery got away with—calling him Avian.

"My door is always open to anyone who wants to come in."

"Anyone? You know very well what's out there. I'd rethink that if I were you."

"Pish, posh. I've been perfectly safe for the fifty-nine years that I've been here. Nothing will harm me as long as the grace of God protects me." At the mention of God, the scars on Avian's back tightened. But he was used to that feeling and barely registered it. "Besides," Father Montgomery continued, "that's why I have you here."

"To protect you if he fails?"

Father Montgomery shuffled over to the refrigerator and pulled out two plates. Turning on the tiny hot plate next to the sink, he peeled off the plastic wrap that covered a slice of meat loaf on each plate. "He works in mysterious ways. I accepted that long ago when you were first brought into my life. Who am I to argue if he wants to send me a personal protector?"

Avian followed him into the kitchen and moved to get the cups that were kept on the second shelf in the cupboard on the left. The shelf Father Montgomery had trouble reaching without his step stool.

"Fifty-nine years. And after all that time, you still won't call me by the name everyone else uses."

"That's because it isn't your name." Father Montgomery glanced over at Avian's right arm, where a multitude of languages inked upon his skin all proclaimed one word: Thirteen. "I know, I know. You have reclaimed that name they gave you so long ago. But when we met, it was another name that God pressed upon my heart: Avian Alexander."

"And it meant absolutely nothing that Alexander was your father's name and that I never would have stopped by the rectory if I hadn't hit that bird with my bike?"

Father Montgomery managed to keep a straight face as he replied, "The resemblance between you and that vulture *was* uncanny."

Avian shook his head, but he didn't hide the brief smile that lifted the corner of his lips. "Speaking of bikes, did you know Pete's Salvage Yard is being guarded by a hellhound?"

"Is it, now?" Father Montgomery paused in the middle of reaching into the fridge again. The smell of warming meat loaf filled the small kitchen. "Any trouble?"

"None that I could see. He said the dog came along with

the junkyard when he inherited it. I'll keep an eye on it while I'm in town, though."

"And how long do you think that will be?" The priest tried not to look too hopeful, but he was failing miserably.

"I have to meet Mint in Louisiana sometime soon, but other than that my schedule's open."

"Is he still running the hotel? He's good people. Helping out those who don't have anywhere else to go."

Mint was a Cajun witch doctor turned hotel proprietor who didn't ask questions of those who needed shelter. Those who Avian was usually on a first-name basis with. When a family of succubi and incubi or passive Wasali demons needed a place to stay for a couple of weeks, Avian sent them to Mint. And when Mint had a couple of bad eggs pass through every now and then, like the Slavic Rumsalkya demons, he sent them on to Avian.

"Yeah, he's still there. Says he wants to retire soon, but we both know that'll never happen."

He sat down at the table as Father Montgomery proudly held up a bottle of ketchup. "Brand new! Sister Serena bought it for me when she went into town last week."

Avian took the bottle, and Father Montgomery put both plates of meat loaf on the table. Avian didn't really care for mortal food (although ketchup *did* make everything taste better), but sharing a meal was something normal people did. And Father Montgomery liked that.

Pretending they were normal.

The priest bowed his head and silently mouthed a prayer before lifting his fork. Then he paused, glancing at Avian over the top of his glasses. "Your coat?"

Avian stood back up and removed the leather duster, turning around to drape it on the back of his chair and revealing the wicked-looking sword still strapped on his back.

"Weapons at the table." The priest tsked.

But Avian just ignored this instruction and sat down again. Father Montgomery knew when he was fighting a losing battle, so he returned to his meal. When Avian had doused his meat loaf in ketchup and taken a bite, the priest finally spoke about the thing weighing heavily on his heart.

"I'm not sure how much longer the church will be able to remain open," he confessed. "Our numbers have been dwindling and our coffers . . . well, they have seen better days."

"Tell me how much you need and I'll get you the money."

Father Montgomery shook his head. "It's not just the money, Avian. Although, I did have to tell Sister Serena that her hours will be completely cut after Christmas. We don't have the funds to pay her even now, but I couldn't let her go right before the holidays."

Avian waited for the priest to continue.

"Even if I were to accept your donation, without a congregation it would simply delay the inevitable. I fear many of our members have started families of their own and moved on." He glanced down at his plate forlornly. "It seems I am a shepherd without a flock."

"That might not be such a bad thing. Don't most humans retire at your age?"

Father Montgomery looked at Avian fondly. "My boy, perhaps you are right. Retirement might be something that I should look at with a fresh perspective."

"I can get a sidecar for the motorcycle," Avian said. "You can travel the world with me."

"Ride in the sidecar? What if I want to drive?"

"You'll have to get your own bike for that. I don't do shotgun."

The priest laughed, and the tension in Avian's gut eased up. Maybe he was wrong. This would be just like every other visit he'd made home, and everything would be fine.

They finished dinner and then had some coffee before Father Montgomery finally shuffled off to his bedroom. Avian was just about to go lock the front door when someone knocked.

Striding across the room, he threw the door open. "Yeah?"

A skinny, bundled-up girl with brown hair stood outside on the front step. Her cheeks were red, a fresh scratch covering one of them. The shadow of an occupying soul flared to life briefly beneath the surface of her face.

She took a step back, startled to see him. "I'm looking for Father Montgomery. I know it's late, but I was hoping he was still up."

"He's not. Do you have any idea what time it is?"

"But the light's on."

"I had to turn a light on because someone felt the need to bang on the door at three thirty in the morning." Avian crossed his arms and scowled. "Do you always stop by for late-night calls?"

"No, I . . . I needed someone to talk to and I figured that he would be . . ." She looked down at the ground and then took a step away. "Just forget it."

"Already forgotten." Avian closed the door behind him hard as that gut feeling of danger hit him again, deep and fast. People like her were trouble. Manipulative, greedy, controlling. Looking to bleed more and more out of people like

Father Montgomery until there would be nothing left. Then she'd move on to find another fix. They always did.

That was the problem with humans who were conduits for the dead.

They were called Echos. And she was one of them.

CHAPTER FIVE

Cyn turned away from the tall, angry-looking guy at the rectory door and put her hands into her pockets. When she saw the face beneath hers reflected in the window at the apartment, she hadn't thought, she'd just reacted. And found herself coming to the church for help. It wasn't like she could really explain to Father Montgomery what was going on, though—she didn't even know herself. She'd learned the hard way when she was seven years old and saw someone else's face looking out from beneath hers for the first time not to tell anyone else exactly what she was seeing.

No one would believe her anyway.

Something brushed against her fingers, and Cyn realized the cop's card was still in her pocket. Unconsciously, she rubbed the sharp corner into a bent nub.

What's he doing here? Does it have anything to do with Hunter's murder?

Her fingers moved from the business card to the gold ring at the thought of Hunter's name, and panic coursed through her. She didn't want to go back to the apartment. It was too dark there. Too cold. Too much room for her thoughts and her headspace and whatever else was taking up real estate inside her body.

She needed a distraction. Something shiny and fast.

Route 202 led out of town, and it was there that Cyn found herself. Thumb raised, looking for a car to steal. A black Mustang came around a curve, and she threw one hip out, cocking her body at an angle.

The car came to a stop, and the middle-aged driver rolled down his window. "Helloooo, midlife crisis," she muttered.

"Need a ride?" he called out.

Cyn walked around to the driver's side and leaned in, pupils dilating. "Sounds like a good idea. How about you give me your keys and get out?"

The man looked up at her, wide-eyed. "Sure." And got out of the car.

"Are you from around here?"

Cyn tried to keep the chances of running into the car owners again at a minimum.

"I live two hours upstate. Just dropping my kids off at their mother's house."

Cyn climbed into the driver's seat and glanced over at the side of the road. The man's breath was showing in frozen puffs of air. It would have to be a short ride tonight. Too cold to leave him out here for long.

"Okay, here's what you're going to do," she said. "Keep following this road, and I'll be back to pick you up in twenty—no, forty minutes, tops."

He turned and started walking down the highway, and Cyn thought she just might be able to make it this time. As long as she drove fast enough, she might be able to chase away her demons for good.

But it was only a couple of minutes later when sounds went dead, her sight grew dim, and her fingers clamped down onto the steering wheel.

Even though she fought it, there was nothing she could do. *He* was taking control.

Suddenly jerking back to awareness, Cyn found herself driving straight toward the edge of a cliff at sixty miles an hour.

She slammed on her brakes, the car fishtailed, and she hooked the wheel sharply to the left. Trying not to panic, she rode it out, letting gravity dictate the direction. Tires skidded on the loose gravel, and her heart stopped as momentum carried her closer and closer to the edge. Finally, with just inches to spare, the car came to a screeching halt.

Her fingers went numb. *Where am I?*

She couldn't remember anything. Couldn't remember where the car had come from or why she'd been careening straight toward certain death.

The door squeaked loudly as she opened it and got out. Leaning her forehead against the cold metal frame, Cyn inhaled slowly. *God, I need a cigarette.* Her hands suddenly started shaking, and she glanced down at them in surprise. A sob clawed its way out of her throat, and she shoved it back down. *Don't cry. Don't start crying now.*

To distract herself, she stepped closer to the edge of the cliff. Stared down into the abyss below. It was so dark and so deep, it reminded her of the night sky when there weren't any stars.

They climbed up onto the bed of the pickup truck. The view was wide and clear, but there weren't any stars. They were still too close to the city. Hunter wrapped his arms around her and leaned in from behind. "I love coming out here like this."

Cyn grinned. "You know what they say. You can take the boy out of the country, but you can't take the country out of the boy."

"Pennsylvania isn't country."

"Since you grew up on a fifty-acre farm there, I'd say that's country."

"Farmette," Hunter corrected. "A hobby farm used on the weekends for overflow crops."

"Did it have a barn?" Cyn leaned in closer to him and felt his head bob up and down. "Did it have a tractor? A truck? A rooster? A cow?"

He nodded his agreement again.

"Then I rest my case. Barn, tractor, cow. F-A-R-M. You are country, country boy."

He lowered his head and spoke softly into her ear. Lips humming against her skin. "You know what they say about country boys, right?"

"What?" Cyn whispered.

"That we have tough hands . . . but soft hearts."

The laughter that suddenly erupted out of Cyn shook both of them. "Oh my God, that was the cheesiest line ever, Hunter." She turned to face him. "Tough hands and soft hearts . . ." She shook her head and he laughed with her.

But their laughter faded as he reached out. Cupping the back of her head, he gently pulled her closer. "Did it work?"

"Yeah." Cyn breathed the words across his lips before she closed the distance between them. "It worked."

Shaking the memory of Hunter off, Cyn stepped back from the edge of the cliff and returned to the car. *Don't think about him now. It's easier not to remember.*

Turning the heater up to full blast, she held her cold fingers up to the vents. She still couldn't remember where she'd been going or who the car belonged to. Reaching for the glove box, She pulled out an insurance card, and everything came rushing back at the sight of James Donnely's name and address.

He was still out there.

She almost stalled out the engine in her haste to back up from the cliff. She didn't want to look at the dashboard clock, but her eyes betrayed her. Almost two hours had passed.

Cyn forgot to breathe as she looked for any sign of James, scanning the edges of the trees bordering the highway. It wasn't until she'd gone six exits down that she finally spotted him. His cheeks and ears were red, but he didn't seem to be any worse for wear.

You got lucky.

"Thanks for letting me borrow your car," Cyn said, coming

to a stop beside him. "Why don't you get in and we'll go grab a cup of coffee before you get on your way back home?"

He nodded absentmindedly, and she let him climb behind the wheel. Once he seemed coherent enough to drive, Cyn directed him to the nearest gas station and pumped him full of hot coffee and stale doughnuts. Then she told him to forget about their little diversion and not stop again until he made it safely home.

As she started to walk the four miles back to her apartment and the sky turned the color of pink ash, the lonely highway stretching out in front of her was a reminder of just how long the trek back was going to be. *Maybe I should flag down another ride.*

But before she could do anything, a car came up behind her.

"Hey," the cop from Sleepy Hollow said, sticking his head out the window. "Need a ride?"

"You didn't call me."

He had to repeat himself because Cyn was concentrating so hard on trying to breathe normally that she didn't hear him the first time.

"Huh? Oh . . . yeah." She forced her fingers to relax their death grip on the door handle. "Sorry. I don't have a cell phone."

She made her shoulders move up and down in what she hoped was a convincing shrug.

He guided the car toward the Hampton Falls exit ramp, and Cyn silently counted down the seconds until she could make her escape. *Just hold it together a little bit longer.*

"Why would you want me to call you anyway?" Only two more stoplights to make it through. Time to stop letting him ask all the questions.

She even managed a grin.

"Since I'm here on vacation, I thought you could show me around."

Is he trying to ask me out on a date?

Cyn pulled down the back of her wig and looked out the window. The diner was straight ahead. "You can just drop me off up here."

"At the diner?"

"Yeah."

"Why don't I take you home?"

Cyn wasn't about to lead him straight to where she lived. He might be just a harmless guy asking her for a date, but he was still a cop. "I'm meeting a friend for breakfast. So ... thanks ..."

"Declan," he reminded her.

"*Right.* Declan." He pulled into the parking lot, and Cyn

had to remind herself *not* to go running from the car the instant he stopped.

"No problem. Just be careful."

Cyn paused, one hand on the door handle. "Be careful?"

"The first time we met, that kid was being an asshole to you, and now, the second time, you were stranded on the side of a highway."

Cyn forced a smile. "I guess it's a good thing you're here, then." She got out of the car before he could reply but returned his wave when he pulled away.

"Yup. It's totally a good thing that a cop from Sleepy Hollow is here in Hampton Falls," she said under her breath as his taillights grew smaller and smaller in the distance. "Nothing could make me happier."

CHAPTER SIX

Y ou look like shit. Get any sleep today?" Lenny tossed a
pile of cold cigarette butts from the bucket next to the
back door and sat down on the stoop, wedging a phone book
under the door to keep it open.

"Yeah. Tons. Can't you tell by my bloodshot eyes that I got more
than my fair share of beauty sleep?" Cyn tied her apron on and left
the strings tangled. It was time for her shift, and she was beyond
tired. After Declan had left, she'd hung around until the locker
room opened at eight and then took a quick shower before heading back to her apartment. She'd tried to get some sleep but had
been too wired to actually close her eyes for anything more than
ten minutes at a time. "It was fucking great. I slept like a queen."

Lenny shook his head at her tone and held out one of his cigarettes in a peace offering.

"I'm trying to quit."

But her hand was reaching for it even as she said those words.

"I've quit before too. Twice." Lenny flicked open his lighter and she leaned in. "Sometimes a good smoke is what you need to keep the nightmares at bay."

His eyes shifted away from her, and Cyn realized that he might have some demons of his own. They sat in silence until she finished puffing.

"Hey, I'm here if you ever want to . . . you know." Lenny shrugged.

Cyn pretended she didn't hear him.

"Thanks for the cigarette," she said instead. "You've officially broken my quitting streak."

Lenny grinned as he held up both middle fingers and flipped her off, a fresh smoke stuck between his lips. Cyn straightened her wig—brunette again tonight—and headed in to greet the customers.

Three and a half hours later, only two customers had come in, and one of them ordered a slice of pie. Not even coffee or a soft drink to go with it. Just pie. And he was a cheapskate to boot.

Cyn didn't bother to use her mind mojo on him. If she kept making the customers leave five-dollar tips on two-dollar checks, someone was bound to start noticing. Lenny had already made a point to mention all the green she was bringing home.

In between breaks, she snuck a couple more cigarettes and tried not to doze off. But it was a fight she was losing, and Marv caught her using her coat as a pillow behind the front counter.

"I'm not paying you to sleep here. That's what you have a bed for. If you're really that tired, go home."

She couldn't go home to her bed even if she wanted to. She didn't have one.

Stuffing her coat behind a box of extra napkins, she acted like she was counting them. "I can't hear you. I'm too busy working."

"Working, my ass." Marv grabbed a dust broom and pushed it across the floor. "I see that again, and you're done."

Cyn poured on the charm. "Come on, Marv. Don't be like that. You know I need the money." He liked it when she acted like he was doing her a huge favor, when in reality he couldn't get any other waitress to work the night shift, because he was so cheap.

Lucky for him, she was desperate.

"*Work.* Don't sleep."

Cyn stuffed a handful of napkins into the front pocket of her uniform. Functioning on autopilot, she checked the holder on each table and refilled the ones that were almost empty. It was another hour before the bell over the door jingled again.

She didn't bother looking up from the crossword puzzle she was halfheartedly filling in as she said, "Sit wherever you like. The floor's open."

Then she saw it was the cop from Sleepy Hollow again. *Declan.*

He had one finger on his menu like he was considering his choices, but he was watching her instead. Sitting at table seven. Next to the back door.

Cyn's throat went dry, and she had to cough to clear it. Why was he here? To ask her out on a date?

Stay calm. Take his order. It's no big deal.

She picked up the coffeepot and put on her brightest smile. "Would you like a cup?"

Her hand only trembled a little bit.

"Sure thing." His grin was big and bright too. "So we meet again."

"I guess that's what happens when you come into the diner where I work." *For the second time.* But she made sure to give him a flirtatious wink.

He glanced down at the menu. "I'm thinking about the soup. What's the special of the day?"

"Clam chowder."

"What are your other soup choices?"

"Clam chowder or clam chowder."

Marv liked to keep things simple. He was always spouting off about picking one thing and doing it well. "I know, not very much of a choice." Cyn gave him a sympathetic eye roll. "But it's the best clam chowder you'll ever taste. I can promise you that."

"If it's even half as good as the crabs at Tom's Crab Shack, then I'll take it."

"You went?"

He nodded.

"Glad to hear it." She put on an I'm-so-happy-you-took-my-suggestion face. "So one order of clam chowder. Will that be all? Or do you want some more time to look at the menu and—"

"Have you been by the Crab Shack recently?"

Cyn's grip on the coffeepot handle tightened. "I'm not really a big seafood person." The back of her wig itched, but she ignored it. "So I don't remember exactly."

"It's just that I couldn't get the all-you-can-eat special. I asked about it, and Tom himself told me they haven't had it since June. Stopped because it was costing them too much money."

The coffeepot almost slipped out of her hands.

Shit, she was screwed. She was so fucking screwed. That must have been an old takeout menu she'd found on the floor of her building.

Suddenly, Cyn would have given just about anything for several of her buttons to spontaneously start popping open. Hell, she wouldn't be averse to flashing him *and* Marv and Lenny just to give him something else to think about.

The cop leaned back in his seat, legs stretched out in front of him, hands resting on the table. "I mean, look, I understand," he said. "When you're local to these parts, you don't always go out to eat as often as someone just passing through."

Cyn smoothed down the back of her wig and forced a smile as her brain worked feverishly, trying to come up with an explanation. The sound of Lenny bringing out a tub full of dishes came from behind her. But before she could say anything, Lenny spoke up.

"Cyn? She's not a local. She's only been here for, what, a couple of months now?" He had a dirty towel slung over his left shoulder, and both hands gripped the plastic tub. Cyn's smile turned to a grimace, and a bead of sweat rolled down between her shoulder blades.

"Only a couple of months?" The cop turned his sharp gaze toward Lenny. "You don't say."

CHAPTER SEVEN

The second night that Avian was home, he sat staring into the fireplace long after Father Montgomery had gone to bed. He could barely feel the heat it was giving off. Thanks to his . . . *heritage*, hot and cold were things he had a hard time distinguishing. Made it a real bitch if he wasn't careful. More than once, he'd risked losing a finger to frostbite.

But the fire was a welcome distraction. He still couldn't shake the underlying feeling of danger, and he wondered if it had anything to do with that Echo.

I need a drink.

Avian stood up to go check the kitchen, knowing that he

wouldn't find anything in there stronger than cooking sherry. Which worked in a pinch. He'd admit to drinking worse. The liquor cooked up during the Prohibition-era days was right up there on the "worse" list. A mix of rotten corn mash and back-alley gasoline, it made paint thinner taste like fine bourbon.

Bourbon. That sounds good.

Cash would have some down at the Black Cadillac.

He passed a twenty-four-hour diner on the way to the bar, and then the alley where he'd come upon a Grenabli demon/vampire fight late last night. Damn vampire had had a bull head with horns. Must have been part of the Navarro coven from Spain. He'd heard about their experimentations with drinking bull's blood in order to make themselves stronger and become truly immortal.

Guess they'd have to work a little harder at that whole immortality thing.

He parked his motorcycle and went into the bar, automatically taking in the fact that there were eight people inside. All bikers. And all one hundred percent human.

Cash was drying off a glass when Avian entered but immediately came over to greet him. "Thirteen! Always a pleasure to have you grace our presence."

Cash *wasn't* one hundred percent human. But he made sure

to let Avian know a long time ago where his loyalties were.

Avian took his outstretched hand. "Nice to be back home."

Cash flipped the empty glass, and it landed neatly on the bar, upside down. Without even asking, he reached for a bottle of Buffalo Trace bourbon.

Avian glanced around the room. The bar hadn't changed much since the last time he'd been here. Same Johnny Cash memorabilia plastering the walls, a couple of large-screen TVs, and a jukebox that had seen better days. But there was a new addition hanging above one of the pool tables: a framed pool stick splintered into two pieces.

"Arts-and-craft times, huh, Cash?" He gestured over at the hanging cue.

Cash placed an amber-colored bottle and a glass filled with ice in front of him. "Since that was the thing that came between us, literally, when you saved my life, I figured I should give it a place of honor. Still chaps my ass that I owe you one for that."

"You could have handled that succubus without me."

Cash laughed and shook his head. "Yeah, I don't think so. At least not while she was trying to eat my liver."

"Still sore?"

Cash rubbed his side, and a pained expression came over

his face. "Damn doctor sewed me up with a fishhook and twine. Left one hell of a scar."

Avian poured just enough bourbon to cover the bottom of his glass. "Chicks dig scars. Didn't anyone ever tell you that?"

"That's what I keep telling myself. But so far, the ones I keep finding don't."

With a rueful grin, Cash headed back to his bartending duties, and Avian took a slow sip of his bourbon. Savoring the taste as the liquor burned a straight shot through him. This was exactly what he needed after a year spent on the road. Granted, a human year was like a blink of an eye to him. But even he got tired of the daily grind of chasing down baddies who didn't want to play nice with humans day in and day out.

Then the door opened, and the girl who'd stopped by Father Montgomery's house came walking in. She was wearing some kind of waitress uniform and didn't have a coat on.

"Whiskey. Jack Daniels," she said from the far end of the counter. "Or whatever you've got." Her pupils dilated, and she stared at Cash with the obvious intent of trying to make him give her what she wanted.

Cash took her in slowly, but shook his head. "Nope."

Confusion crossed her face. Then she tried again. "I want some whiskey. *Now.*"

Avian took another sip of his bourbon and watched their interaction bemusedly. He'd seen this before with Frank Rooney—another Echo—back in 1928. One of the souls inside Rooney had come from a voodoo priestess who had a lot of power. Rooney was able to tap into that power as well and compelled people to give him things. He used it on bank tellers. Stole three million dollars before Avian found him and made him give it back.

The girl stared down Cash.

Won't take, Avian thought. *That only works on humans.*

"I've got an ID," she finally said, digging in her pocket. "Here. See?"

Cash leaned in to get a closer look. "Uh-huh. So you're twenty-nine?"

"I'm whatever age you need me to be to get some of that whiskey," she said in a low voice.

Avian picked up his glass. Cash glanced at him as he moved closer, and Avian gave him a brief nod. Cash reached for the square Jack Daniels bottle and poured her a shot.

The girl finally noticed him and glared as she took the glass. "Oh, nice. The guy who wouldn't let me see Father Montgomery. Are you stalking me now? Back off, asshole. I'm not in the mood."

Avian grinned at her attitude. "You know I'm the only rea-son you're going to be drinking at all tonight, right?"

She gulped down the whiskey in one smooth motion and slammed the glass down on the counter. "Yeah. Okay. Go right on ahead and keep thinking that, douche bag." Then she turned back to Cash. "I'll have another."

Chapter Eight

It took four shots of whiskey before Cyn was able to relax and stop thinking about Declan and wondering why he was here. After Lenny had let it slip that she was new in town, she'd told Marv she wasn't feeling well and wanted to go home. Then she slipped out the door in the kitchen, leaving her coat out on the floor. She wasn't about to go back and get it.

She slid the empty shot glass down the bar counter and giggled a little when it bumped the wall then fell off. It didn't break, though, because the asshole from Father Montgomery's house reached out and caught it.

"Hey, that's a nice catch," she said in spite of herself. He palmed the shot glass and then made it reappear on the bar.

Cyn blinked once and squinted at him. "How'd you do that?"

He didn't answer but shook his head when she opened her mouth to call for another round. For some reason, this really irritated her—who was *he* to stop her from getting another drink?—and she gave him her dirtiest look. "I'll have one more," she said loudly.

"No you won't," he replied. "You've had enough."

"Excuse me?" She tried again. Louder this time. "*One more, please. Over here.*"

The guy exchanged looks with the bartender, and then the bartender ignored her.

"It's not gonna happen." Annoying Tall Guy crossed his arms. "But you can keep trying. It's amusing."

Cyn marched over until she was standing directly in front of the bartender. She didn't know why her mind-mojo powers weren't working. All she wanted to do was keep drinking. It made everything nice and hazy, so she didn't have to think all the time.

Cyn willed the bartender to give her another shot, but it was a useless act. He kept ignoring her.

"Fine," Cyn said. If the asshole was somehow responsible for this, then he owed her. And she was going to take that almost-full bottle of Buffalo Trace sitting next to him as payment.

Cyn shot past him and grabbed for the bottle. Two full swigs of it were down the hatch before she felt his hand on her arm. Stopping her.

"Why don't we find a quiet table," he said. "Come with me."

She didn't know why, but for some reason she found herself following him.

Maybe it was because he let her hold on to the bottle of bourbon.

They headed for the far corner, where the people sitting at a table suddenly seemed interested in playing a game of pool on the opposite side of the bar and cleared out. Cyn picked at the peeling label on the front of the bottle as they took the recently vacated seats.

"So, what do you want to talk about?" she asked.

"Why don't you start with what's going on."

"What do you mean, what's going on? Haven't you ever seen someone get drunk before?"

"Yeah, but that's not what this is. And that's not who you are." He tilted his head to the side and studied her. Cyn realized that his eyes were the darkest shade of brown she'd ever seen.

"You don't know me. So how can you think you know what 'this is'?" Cyn lifted the bottle to her lips. "I'm just a drunk teenager with a fake ID in a crappy bar. That's it."

"Don't let Cash hear you talking shit about his place, or it's the last time you'll ever see the inside of it."

She paused before taking a sip. "Seriously?" Then she laughed at him. "You think I'm afraid of being thrown out of *here?*" She glanced around. "The floor is covered in stains that look like they're either vomit or . . . or . . . some kind of bile or something, and—"

"It's blood."

"Oh, *excuse me.*" She waved the bottle around. "How nice. The floor is covered in *bloodstains.* That totally makes it authentic. And what's with all of these pictures of the same guy on the wall? Shouldn't there be *Sports Illustrated* swimsuit models, or Victoria's Secret posters? This is a biker bar, isn't it?"

"It's a Johnny Cash–themed bar. Hence the Johnny Cash memorabilia."

"Gotcha." Cyn cocked her finger at him like she was taking aim and then pulled the trigger. "I guess that's where the name Cash comes from too."

"No, that's his real name. Warren Cash."

"Riiiight. Okay, well I think that's enough talking for now. This is a ridiculous conversation, and I just want to get wasted in peace, okay? I'm not looking for anything more than that."

"Why?"

"Why do I want to get wasted? Or why do I want to do it in peace? Because both questions have the same answer: It's been a shitty couple of days."

Cyn wasn't paying attention to the other people in the room until there was the distinct sound of footsteps coming to a stop behind her. She turned around to see who it was.

A squat guy with a blond crew cut and no neck, whose muscles rippled up beneath both arms of his Ed Hardy T-shirt, stared at her table companion. "Thirteen," he said. "It's been a while."

One of his arms suddenly split wide open, revealing a moving maw beneath the gaping flesh. It was lined with little suckers—like a miniature octopus tentacle—and it was hideous.

Cyn recoiled for an instant before regaining her composure.

"Bryn," her table companion replied, "I thought we had an agreement. You don't come back in here again, and I don't kill you."

"I've worked out some new terms." No-neck's arm made a squealing noise, like a hungry baby piglet waiting to be fed.

"Too bad for you I don't renegotiate my contracts." He looked down at No-neck's moving arm. "You should think about feeding that thing, though. Looks cranky."

Cyn felt her jaw hit the floor as she turned back to the guy who had been so calmly sitting next to her. "You can *see* that?!"

"Of course I can," he replied. "And now I'm going to get rid of it."

CHAPTER NINE

The rest of the bar patrons seemed oblivious to what was about to happen right in front of them, but Cash wasn't. "You know the rules," he said. "Take it outside."

Within the blink of an eye, the two guys in front of her were heading for the alley out back, and Cyn scrambled to follow.

"Don't make too much of a mess out there," Cash called.

"No promises," Avian called back.

No-neck made it to the alley first. He put up his fists in a classic fighting stance and bounced back and forth on the balls of his feet.

"Old school," Avian said. "You know I like it that way."

"Whatever it takes to kick your ass. That's the way *I* like it."

Avian didn't assume a fighting stance but started taking off his leather jacket. Cyn was momentarily distracted by the sleeve of ink covering his right arm. She could also see something strapped between his shoulder blades. Taking his time to neatly fold the jacket, he set it off to the side, then simply walked up and punched No-neck in the head.

No-neck returned the jab, only lower, and hit Avian's stomach.

Avian didn't even flinch. "Is that it? You'll have to hit harder than that if you want to leave a mark." His tone was long and drawn out, taunting just by its even keel.

No-neck reacted with a flurry of punches to Avian's head and shoulders, his head bent low.

With No-neck's head left unguarded, Avian drove his elbow into the back of his skull so hard, Cyn could hear bone crack. No-neck fell back, stunned.

Avian moved fast, striking again, and No-neck fell to his knees. "Damn it," he panted, hands flat against the pavement, arm muscles tensing. "I'm tired of playing this game with you, Thirteen." His biceps split open, and gaping tentacles at least three feet long uncoiled from each one. He flung them like whips and they hurtled with blinding speed, rushing for Avian's face.

One of the tentacle arms shot past Avian, but the other wrapped around his head. The wet suction noise it made turned Cyn's stomach. As soon as the arm had gotten a hold, its little suckers opened wide and produced rows of shiny teeth. Gnashing and biting, they immediately stripped away anything they came in contact with. Little hunks of skin the size of fleshy Band-Aids were pulled from Avian's cheek as the tiny carnivores started devouring him inch by inch.

The second tentacle tried to wrap around his waist, but Avian moved out of the way. With his free hand, he reached behind him and pulled out a wicked-looking double-edged sword from the strap between his shoulder blades. The sword sliced through the tentacle arm, but it didn't lose its suction grip on his face.

Suddenly, Avian threw his sword straight up into the air as hard as he could.

With both hands now free, he ripped off the tentacle arm and tossed it at No-neck. No-neck screamed as the gaping mouths latched onto his head and immediately started slurping.

But No-neck wasn't finished yet, and even half-blinded by

his own appendage, he pulled back and lashed out again with his remaining tentacle. This time he went for Avian's feet.

Cyn couldn't help herself. "Watch out!" she screamed. "He's going for your—"

A whistling noise split the air as the sword came crashing back down to earth.

In that split second, Avian glanced over at Cyn and the sword fell blade down, just out of his reach.

The look he gave her was so full of rage that she almost saw smoke come out of his nose.

As the tentacle fell short of Avian's feet, he dropped to the ground. When he lifted his head again, the sword was in his hand and his eyes were red. Even in the shadows, Cyn could see that. And the smoke? It was coming from his *skin*.

She could see his arms more clearly now, and they were covered in scars that stood out in sharp contrast against the black ink of his tattoos. Rigid and bumpy, they were milky white in color. Although they weren't scars, exactly. They were more like burns.

His back muscles strained against his dark T-shirt as he lifted the sword, and she could see the raised outline of burn tissue there, too.

With a final heave, Avian lunged toward No-neck, who

was still struggling against his own tentacle, and swung the blade down. The sword slid through No-neck's body like butter, and Avian followed the trajectory by falling to one knee.

No-neck wavered for an instant, then split into two pieces.

The tentacle arm that was attached to No-neck immediately pulled back as all of the life left its host, while the arm on his head shriveled up like a piece of puckered skin jerky.

Cyn briefly wondered if any of the people in the bar were going to come see what had just happened. But even if they did, she knew they wouldn't see anything beyond two guys engaged in a bar fight.

They wouldn't see a weird octopus-arm man. Or a guy who had red eyes and smoke coming off of him, like she did.

The winner of the fight was still clutching the handle of his sword and bent down on the ground. Cyn hesitantly walked over to him. Smoke curled off of him like steam, and she didn't want to get too close. His shoulder-length dark hair fell around his face, revealing the nape of his neck and the large "13" tattooed there.

Wasn't that what Octopus Guy called him? Thirteen?

"Um, Thirteen? Are you okay?"

"Don't touch me." His voice was barely recognizable.

"Wasn't planning on it."

One of the burn marks on his arm deepened, and she stared at it. It looked like it was burning its way *through* his skin. From the inside out.

Then he looked up and she saw the horns.

CHAPTER TEN

Avian had to give the girl some credit—she didn't lean over and throw up before passing out at the sight of his slice and dice with Bryn. She was just fine with that. It was the sight of *him* that did it to her.

Getting to his feet, Avian slid his sword into its scabbard and put his coat back on. Then he glanced down at his boots. One of those suck-mouth bastards had managed to strip away a good chunk of the sole. He'd have to get that fixed before he left town.

The scars on his back burned a bit less now, but he knew it was still too dangerous to go near her. "Cash!" he yelled. "Get out here."

Cash appeared an instant later and took in Bryn's mangled body with the same nonchalance he would have if there was some trash ready to be taken out. "I'll take care of it," he said. "Don't worry."

"Not him. *Her.*" He gestured to the girl lying inelegantly next to a pile of puke. "Can you put her up for a couple of hours? I just need some time to cool down."

"Want me to take her home?"

"No. I'll do it. She's an Echo."

Cash gazed at her. "Shiiiit. I've only met one of those before. I didn't see it."

"The last one I came across was Shelley. It's been a while for me, too."

The ache in Thirteen's voice was a wound that still hadn't healed, even after all this time. And Cash knew better than to bring up old memories.

"I'll put her in the supply room. I've got an extra blanket in there. She'll be fine."

"Thanks. I'll be back as soon as I can."

He went to the roof of the church. Just like he always did when the fire inside got to be too much. Father Montgomery had invited him to come inside more than once, but the demon part of him *really* didn't like that idea. The other side of him yearned for a higher connection. This was as close to a compromise as he was willing to make.

Perched among the roof eaves, Avian watched the clouds change and the sky lighten. He knew what he looked like fresh after a fight. More monster than man, it was enough to scare anyone away. A fact he often used to his advantage.

Eventually, the scars on his back would recede and his horns would retract. But the nubs never fully went away. Concentrating on the color of his eyes, he changed them so that any remaining red would be hidden by a glamour. He always chose brown to blend in. His skin repaired itself—the tiny rips and tears stitching back together. But he left the scar under his left ear.

It was the only thing he had to remember Shelley by.

When he was sure that everything was under control again, he made his way back to the Black Cadillac. It was closed, but Cash let him inside and gestured to the back room. "Sleeping like a baby. Never woke up."

Avian leaned over the girl and touched her forehead. Like the other Revenants, he could read memories. He traced back through her day to see where she lived and recognized a building that used to be a printing place. She weighed nothing in his arms, so he left his motorcycle at the bar and carried her the couple of blocks there.

The building had a vacant look to it, and there wasn't a lock on the door. Which wasn't strictly necessary in this part of town but was stupid any way you looked at it. A string brushed the side of his face as he entered the empty room, and he pulled on it. A single bulb flared to life.

A sleeping bag in the corner, a rusty heater, and an open suitcase were obvious signs that someone was living there, but at best it could only be described as spartan. There was no bed, no kitchen. Not even a shower, from what he could see. The only thing she did seem to have an abundance of was plants. There were a bunch of dead ones lined up against the windows.

"You better hope one of those souls inside of you has a green thumb that you just haven't tapped into yet, because it looks like you're going to need it," he said out loud.

She didn't stir.

Dumping her onto the sleeping bag, he took another look around the grim space. Even the most basic room Mint had to offer at his hotel looked luxurious compared with this. Was this why she was at the bar? Trying to drown her sorrows over a troubled home life?

He almost felt a moment of pity for her, but then it passed. She was an Echo. She'd find someone else to manipulate into setting her up with something new. Echoes didn't seem to have any trouble with things like that.

The sun was almost up, and Father Montgomery was waiting for him when Avian got back to the rectory, so they sat down for an early-morning cup of coffee.

"Were you out all night?" Father Montgomery asked. "I have your old cello in the church. Perhaps that might help?"

The priest could always tell when he'd had a busy evening.

"You know I haven't played in years. I just went to a bar and ended up taking out some garbage."

"Sounds like a normal evening for you, then."

Father Montgomery knew what Avian did, was well aware of what was out there. But they never talked about the side of him that flared up at the end of the fight. The demon part Avian had struggled with for so long.

It had been. Except there was something that still bothered Avian. That nagging feeling in his gut. He glanced over at the priest. "A girl came by here the other night. She wanted to see you. It was late, though, and she left."

"What did she look like?"

"I don't know. You humans all look alike to me. She was younger, with brown hair. Lives in an abandoned building a couple of blocks from the bar. Has a bunch of plants."

"Ah, yes." Father Montgomery shook his head. "Her name is Cyn. She's stopped by to see me a couple of times at the church. Likes to talk about her plants."

"She came into the bar tonight too. Seems to be running from something." Avian's large hands wrapped around his coffee cup, overlapping each other. "You need to be careful, Father. She's an Echo."

Avian rarely called him that. It was usually Father Montgomery, or "priest." But in that small, simple word his true feelings were revealed.

"Maybe she's running from that and doesn't realize it. Did you have the chance to . . . ?" Father Montgomery gestured to his forehead.

"Read her memories? Nothing beyond where she lives. She was incapacitated, so I just dropped her off."

Father Montgomery frowned and gazed down into his drink. "I think she needs help. She hasn't come right out and asked for it, but it's there nonetheless."

"I'm sure she'll find someone else to give her what she wants. But it's not going to be you."

"You know my door is always open to those in need, Avian. As long as—"

"That doesn't apply to Echos. I've told you before what they're capable of."

"Shelley was an Echo, and she didn't take advantage."

Avian's grip tightened. "Shelley wasn't like the others."

Father Montgomery glanced up at the subtle shift in Avian's tone. "You're right, of course. But my vows require me to help my fellow man, and that's something I take quite seriously."

"Then let me put your mind at ease, Father." Avian stood up. "This time I'll take care of it."

CHAPTER ELEVEN

When Cyn woke up, she had no idea how she'd gotten home from the bar and why she was lying on top of the sleeping bag instead of in it. Sunlight was streaming through the windows, but the room was *freezing*. She flipped the switch for the heater, and it started making a ticking sound. She didn't know how much longer it would last, but the front coils slowly began to turn orange.

Her mouth tasted terrible, and she grabbed a second pair of socks before padding into the bathroom. The tap wasn't usable, but she kept a bottle of water by the sink to brush her teeth. A small mirror hung on the wall, and she glanced at it as she passed by.

That face was there beneath hers again.

Cyn gripped the edges of the sink. "Go away," she said. "I don't want you here. This is *my* body, and you can't have it!"

But that smug bastard used her own face against her—the blackened teeth projected like a ghostly image beneath her skin and split into a parody of a smile. She felt that sudden pull of darkness begin to wash over her, and she gripped the sink even harder. "No!"

Cyn fought him with everything she had. She didn't want to black out and wake up to find herself on the edge of a cliff again.

Or surrounded by someone else's blood.

Her head felt like it was splitting open, and she screamed at the intensity. The edges of her vision started to blur, and a feeling like cotton balls being wedged inside her ears made every sound go mute. Her grip loosened, and then she was gone.

The darkness was all wrong in the room when she opened her eyes. It felt more like early morning than late evening. But the alarm hadn't gone off. Cyn remembered that she wasn't scheduled to work tonight, though, so it wasn't like she was missing her shift if she'd overslept.

Groping for the clock next to her bed, Cyn's fingers bumped the edge of something hard. And cold.

Come to think of it, *she* was lying on something hard and cold.

There was an odd smell around her. Like old metal. And what should have been the warm fleece lining of a sleeping bag beneath her fingertips was instead cracked tile. She opened her eyes all the way and saw streaks of dried blood in front of her.

Oh God. Oh my God. Did it happen again? Where am I? Who did I hurt this time?

Slowly, recognition dawned, and she realized that she was lying in the single-stall bathroom of her building. A permanently stained sink and a dirty toilet were the only fixtures, along with a faded black and white tiled floor.

Raising shaking hands to touch her face, Cyn held a jagged piece of tile in her left palm. She dropped it, and it bounced on the floor before coming to a stop.

Glancing down at her arms, Cyn saw right away where the blood had come from. Clotted streaks and crude gashes made a macabre road map of connect-the-dots up and down the translucent veins that pulsed beneath her skin. Dried blood covered the wall and the base of the sink she was lying in front of.

Apparently, in her sleep she'd somehow managed to come into the bathroom, pry up a piece of loose floor tile, and use its rough edge to try to slit her wrists.

"No, no, no, no, no . . ." Hysteria bubbled up, and all she could see in her mind was the blood all over Hunter. "This can't happen again!"

Cyn got to her feet, and the room dipped sideways. She was light headed. But she couldn't tell if that was due to blood loss or because she couldn't remember the last time she'd had something to eat.

She turned on the faucet, and it spewed dark and dirty water. She didn't like the idea of washing up with it, but she didn't have any choice. There wasn't enough bottled water left.

Gingerly wiping the open edges of the cuts with a wad of tissue, Cyn used as little of the dirty water as she could. Wincing at the sight more than the pain, she dried her arms and took in her injuries. There were so many of them. Mostly shallow cuts. Although two were deep enough to be worried about.

Even though her next shift at the diner wasn't until tomorrow night, Cyn knew she couldn't wait that long. She needed a first-aid kit and some bandages. Remembering that she'd left her coat at work too—another reason to go there—Cyn slowly eased her way over to her suitcase to grab a sweater and headed out.

~ ~ ~

Cyn walked to the diner, battling her thoughts every step of the way.

You deserved this, you know. Something inside you is trying to see that you are punished. Which is only fair. You killed your boy-friend in his sleep.

She put both hands over her ears as if to block out her thoughts, but it didn't work. They just kept coming.

His poor family. They'll never know what happened. How could you just leave him there like that? And you claim you loved *him?*

Maybe it was time to run again. With the cop here now, and the blackouts starting again. Maybe it was time to just get out. A couple more days of working at the diner, and then she would take her money and leave this town behind.

God, I hope I can last that long.

The kitchen was empty as Cyn snuck in the back door, and she pocketed a pack of Lenny's cigarettes left out on the prep table. "Sorry, big guy," she said to the empty room. "But I need these more than you do right now. I'll get you another pack. I swear."

The first-aid kit was in the employee bathroom, and she made sure to lock the door behind her before carefully rolling up her sleeves. She didn't see the tube of ointment that was sup-posed to prevent scar tissue until she'd already bandaged half a dozen of the cuts. *That's okay. Maybe I deserve a couple of scars.*

Cyn washed her hands and looked into the mirror. An uneasiness still hung about her. She could see it in the haunted look in her eyes. "I'm not going to let you win, you bastard," she whispered to her reflection. "You hear me? Whoever you are in there, I'm not going to let you win."

She didn't realize then that it was already too late.

CHAPTER TWELVE

Cyn reached for a paper towel to dry off her hands and saw her fingers were covered in mud. Headlights from an empty car sitting nearby provided illumination, revealing that she wasn't in the employee bathroom at the diner anymore, she was in the woods.

Her jeans were slimy and wet, and she was sitting next to a half-dug muddy hole. An empty bottle of Jack was at her feet.

Surprisingly, Cyn took everything in with a sense of extreme calm. She must have had another blackout. Since no one else was in the car, she'd obviously stolen it. Then she . . . *what?* Had some sort of accident?

Getting to her feet, she took a quick walk around the car.

There was a small dent in the bumper. *Okay. Accident it was.* But if it was just an accident, what did she hit? And why was she so dirty?

Then she saw something submerged in the muddy hole. It looked like some sort of stick.

With a sick twisting in her gut, Cyn knew then that she'd hit someone. She'd blacked out again, stolen a car, and hit someone. Then she'd tried to cover it up by digging a hole and burying him.

Dropping to the ground, Cyn crawled on her hands and knees. Paying no attention to the mud that splashed her face, all she could think about was saving him. Saving this man that she'd hit who must have a wife and a family and a pet golden retriever who was patiently waiting by the front door for his master to come home.

"Please be okay. I'll do anything. Just please . . . be okay."

The stick was positioned at an odd angle, and as she reached for it some part of her registered that it wasn't a stick at all. It was covered in fur and had a hoof attached to it. She had to stand in order to gain some leverage to hoist it out of the hole.

The mud made a sucking sound when she pulled, and Cyn grunted, feeling her balance start to shift as the mud gave way and whatever it was in that hole slowly started to move toward her. She pulled as hard as she could and almost lost her grip before falling to her knees.

The mud held on for a second longer, then finally relented, and a dead baby deer slid out of the hole.

It's not a person! I didn't hit anyone!

But her joy was short lived. The little deer was so tiny. The poor thing's leg hung crookedly, obviously this was how she'd dented the bumper. There didn't seem to be any damage to the rest of its body, though, and a broken leg certainly shouldn't have been enough to kill it. *Punctured lung, maybe? Broken neck?*

Then she saw the battered head.

Oh, God. She'd killed it. She was a monster.

Cyn began trembling violently, then leaned over and vomited what small amount of liquid was left in her stomach. She heaved again and again, desperately trying to purge itself. The strength in her arms finally gave out, and she collapsed into the hole.

Covered in wet, slimy mud, Cyn willed herself to give up. To go ahead and die right there. Hopefully she'd freeze to death before she starved, but either way, it was no worse than what she deserved. She'd gone from killing Hunter to killing innocent animals.

But as hard as she tried, she couldn't envision any bright

light to walk into. Or a pit of fire and brimstone, for that matter. Life was refusing to let go, and the only thing she could think of was that she had to get to Father Montgomery.

Maybe he would know what was happening to her.

Cyn rolled over and pulled herself out of the mud inch by painful inch. "I'm sorry," she whispered to the baby deer as she got to her feet. "I'm so, so sorry. Forgive me."

Her sense of direction was skewed, but she started walking anyway. Leaving the car behind. She didn't know who it belonged to, and she didn't want to get caught up in another mess. Eventually she recognized the road she was on and made her way to Father Montgomery's church.

She was filthy when she staggered up to the door of the rectory. Her fingernails ragged and caked with mud. The single act of lifting a shaking hand to ring the bell took all of her remaining strength, and she slid against the door frame, crumpling into a ball.

When he opened the door and glanced down at her in concern, all Cyn could say was, "I killed it. God help me, Father, I killed it. There's something wrong with me. I think I'm possessed."

CHAPTER THIRTEEN

Avian was on his way to Pete's junkyard to see about replacing the muffler on his bike when he noticed the car that had been following him the entire way suddenly turned off. Glancing in his side mirror, he saw a young-looking guy get out and immediately survey his surroundings. Shoulders straight, head held high, he had an air of authority about him. And he was packing. Avian could see the bulge of a holster under his arm.

Law enforcement.

The cop went into a diner, but something didn't feel right about him, so Avian parked and went into the diner too. He watched as the cop sat near the back, which had a full view of the place, and flashed his badge to an overeager waitress who came to take his order.

"Hey, I was wondering if you could do me a favor?" the cop asked.

"Sure. Name it." The waitress licked her lips and then blushed.

"I was in here a couple of nights ago, and there was another cute little waitress. You two could have been sisters. Do you happen to know her name?"

The waitress frowned, not sure if he was as interested in her as she wanted him to be. "You mean Cyn? She's the only one that works the night shift. Except for Dougie Ray on her nights off. But he's not little, and he's definitely not cute."

"Cyn. That must be it. Cyn . . . ?"

"I don't know what her last name is." The waitress put one hand on her hip.

"She forgot her coat when she left, and I have it," he explained. "I wanted to return it to her." He smiled at the waitress, and it worked like a charm.

"Well isn't that just so sweet of you, officer."

"Call me Declan."

"Declan . . . I . . ." She fumbled with her notepad. "Cyn will be in tonight. She works from ten to seven."

"Great. I'll stop back in then. Now, would you get me a piece of pumpkin pie? With whipped cream, if you have any."

"Absolutely." She beamed at him again and then made her way over to Avian. When he only ordered a cup of coffee, she left him with a considerably less than cheerful attitude and returned seconds later with a steaming cup.

Avian sipped slowly, taking note of how many times the cop looked over at him. Three total, in the fifteen minutes he was there. The cop paid a couple more compliments to the waitress and then took the number she slipped him as he stood to leave. But he barely glanced at it before stuffing it into his back pocket.

When the cop went to pay, Avian followed him again. He brushed by him, and Avian caught one of the cop's memories. It was a flash of the girl, Cyn—and the mental image was tinged around the edges with red.

Interesting. . . . What's your connection to an Echo?

The cop was still in the parking lot as Avian exited, and Avian didn't miss the fact that he was checking out his license plate. He started his bike up.

"Looks like a classic," the cop said over the roar of the engine.

"It is."

"Are you a collector?"

Avian thought about the thirty motorcycles in the garage of his Massachusetts house. That probably qualified him as a collector. "You could say that."

The cop smiled. But his eyes were hard. "My brother had a motorcycle too. Nothing as nice as yours, just a ninety-nine Honda Valkyrie. But it was his pride and joy."

Avian took note of the word "was."

The cop turned and got into his car. A rental. "Ride safe."

Avian gave the cop plenty of time to pull out, then tailed him for a while. He kept close to the diner, driving around the block several times like he was looking for something. Two girls came walking down the street, and the cop flashed his badge again, asking if either one of them knew Cyn. Avian didn't miss the flash of anger on his face when the answer was no.

When the cop finally pulled away, he drove straight to a motel and went inside room 223.

The car's a rental, and the hotel room means he isn't local. And Avian would bet every last motorcycle he owned that wherever the cop came from was the same place Cyn came from too.

CHAPTER FOURTEEN

Father Montgomery didn't ask any questions as he shep-
herded Cyn inside the rectory, other than if she needed
immediate medical attention. When she told him no, he
handed her a fluffy white towel, pointed her in the direction of
the bathroom, and gave her privacy while she cleaned up.

Cyn stared at the wall of water, watching dirt run down in
tiny brown rivers and circle round the drain as her fingers grew
wrinkly in the shower. *What if he can't help me?*

She wanted to tell Father Montgomery about the cuts on
her arm, what she'd done to the baby deer, and how she'd found
herself on the edge of the cliff. But she didn't want to talk about
Hunter. And he was a pretty big part of it all.

"Whenever you're ready I have some nice hot coffee brewing," Father Montgomery called politely when he heard the water shut off. "And you'll find a set of clothes on the bed in the spare room."

Cyn dried off and found the oversize sweats and faded black and white flannel shirt in the room next door. The pants were too big—she had to double knot the drawstring in order to keep them from falling down—but she didn't mind.

Her wig was a complete disaster. There wasn't much she could do for it, though, so she just finger combed it and then pulled it on. Father Montgomery was waiting for her down in the kitchen. He had an open Bible beside him on the table but was looking out the window at a squirrel climbing a tree.

"I love watching squirrels," he said. "I know people think they're pests, but God has a plan for them. The nuts they bury will grow into trees, providing life and oxygen and nourishment for our planet. What can seem bothersome to one might just have a different purpose for another."

It didn't take a rocket scientist to figure out that he was alluding to her troubles.

"Father Montgomery, I can't begin to tell you how much I appreciate this," Cyn said slowly. "I know this must seem incredibly strange, me just showing up out of the blue like this, covered in mud. But I can't ask you to—"

"Forgive my interruption, but you aren't asking me to do anything that God has not asked of me. We were put on this earth to help our fellow man, and that includes times of trouble and need. I don't want to presume, but based on our previous conversations, you haven't mentioned any family. . . ."

"I'm not close to them."

"Then, please, let the church help you. Whether you need a place to stay, some clothes to wear, or just a warm meal and a shoulder to lean on. And if it's something more than that, you can tell me. I made a solemn vow before God and man not to reveal anything that is shared in confidence."

For a moment, Cyn could almost see everything play out in front of her. To finally belong somewhere as she confessed her secrets and was forgiven for her sins. But then reality came crashing in.

Although God might be forgiving, the State of New York wouldn't be. Especially when it came to murder.

"I don't think . . ." She shook her head but couldn't finish.

"You can trust me," he said, leaning forward earnestly. "Nothing is unforgivable as long as your heart is in the right place."

She highly doubted *that*.

The defeated look in Cyn's eyes tugged at Father Montgomery's heart. She was so young, and so full of hurt.

"You know," he said, "once I found myself in a difficult situation. I was introduced to someone who, like you, didn't have a support system in his life." Thoughts of the early years with Avian made him smile. "Several people in my congregation questioned whether it was right of me to accept this young man into my care. He was troubled, and they thought he might lead me astray."

Cyn ran her pinky around the edge of her coffee cup as she listened.

"He had an unconventional background, and very little interaction with people who didn't want to take advantage of him, so this made him highly suspicious of me. But over time we came to trust each other and rely on each other, and to this day he is one of the best souls that I have ever known."

"He's not six feet tall and angry looking, is he?" she said sarcastically, thinking about the night she'd first come to try and speak to Father Montgomery and had been rudely rebuffed.

Father Montgomery chuckled. "Avian can be a bit protective, but he has a good heart."

Cyn glanced out the window. Father Montgomery couldn't

help her. He was talking about raising wayward boys with attitude problems. Not murder and suicide attempts and cruelty to animals.

Cyn felt her stomach pitch again at the thought of that poor deer. *I have to get out of here.*

"Thank you for your kindness, Father Montgomery." She stood, leaving her full mug on the table. "I appreciate it more than you'll ever know."

He saw that she wasn't going to say anything more, so he reached for her hand and patted it. "I understand. And my door is open to you day or night when you *are* ready." He pulled a rosary out of his pocket and passed it to her. "Just as a reminder that you are never alone."

Cyn smiled sadly at him but took his gift. "That's the problem in a nutshell, Father. I'm not alone."

CHAPTER FIFTEEN

Clutching the rosary Father Montgomery had given her, Cyn chain smoked Lenny's pack of cigarettes the entire way back to her apartment. Exhaustion was setting in, and she couldn't stop thinking about that baby deer.

Stumbling on the front step, she felt dizzy again and knew she needed to eat something. So she chased a couple of saltines with some flat ginger ale, then curled up in her sleeping bag. Sleep would make everything better. As long as she didn't dream she would wake up with a clear head, and then she could figure out what to do.

But sleep didn't make everything better, and when Cyn woke again her head was pounding. The room went black, and she had to count to ten before her vision cleared. *Mental note: You need to eat more than just crackers.*

She looked at the clock to try and calculate how long it had been since she'd last had a solid meal and saw it was two o'clock in the morning. Her shift was supposed to start four hours ago. Marv probably thought she was a no-show.

"Shit, shit, shit!" Cyn scrambled out of bed, and something clattered to the floor. She must have fallen asleep with the rosary Father Montgomery had given her.

But when Cyn looked down, she saw that it wasn't a holy relic lying on the floor.

It was a knife.

The room started to tilt again, and Cyn bent over and put her head between her knees. *Where did that come from?* "I must have picked it up from the diner," she said out loud. Willing her words to become true.

But there was no way it was from the diner. The knife had an elaborately decorated handle and a wide, flat blade. It looked like a ceremonial dagger.

Visions of realtors suddenly deciding to stop by the building and stumbling upon the knife filled her mind. *That's the last thing I need.* So she picked up the knife and carried it into the bathroom. Then she lifted the lid on the back of the toilet tank and dropped it into the water. It was the only place she could think of to stash it.

Hurrying over to her suitcase, Cyn pulled out a black bobbed wig and then put on her diner uniform. The cuts on her arms were still clearly visible. A long-sleeved T-shirt layered beneath the uniform wasn't her greatest look, but it covered everything up so she wouldn't have to explain why her arms looked the way they did.

Cyn walked as fast as she could to the diner, but Marv blew a gasket when she got there. "Finally decided to join us, huh?" His apron was messier than usual, and he was juggling plates. "I don't know why you even bothered to show up after pulling this shit."

"I'm sorry, Marv. I got sick." She didn't beat around the bush or give him a smart-ass answer.

"Yeah, well, don't be getting any of my customers sick. That's the last thing I need. Now go get your apron on and get out to table seven."

Cyn followed his direction and moved to take care of the table. But her reaction time was off, and she kept messing up. More than one irritated customer had their burger cooked wrong, or a drink not filled fast enough.

"You really are dragging ass tonight," Marv said when

things finally slowed down. "You're not gonna keel over on me, are you? Makes for bad publicity."

Cyn pulled two empty chairs over to the counter and put her feet up. *Let him say something about me sitting down on the job now. I'll tell him where he can stick it.*

"Must be a flu thing going around. I'll be okay."

Marv shook his head, but a worried look crept across his face. He was just about to say something else when the bell above the door chimed. He glanced over. "It's that cop again. He's been looking for you. Think you can handle one more customer?"

Cyn got to her feet. "Sure." She knew she should be worried: The last time he was in here, she bailed on him. But she didn't feel anything.

Maybe this was acceptance. Maybe she was finally coming to terms with what she did.

"Black hair really doesn't suit you," Declan said with a self-assured smile when she stopped at his table. "I preferred the brown."

"Do you know what you'd like to order?" she replied in a monotone.

"Why do you change your hair color so often? You're not trying to hide something, are you?"

"What about something to drink?" Cyn suggested. "Coffee? Tea? Soda . . . ?"

"That all depends on what I'm going to eat. Dessert requires coffee, but something warm, like a bowl of clam chowder, means I'll want something cold to wash it down with."

He grinned at her, but she wasn't in the mood to play games. "I'll just give you another minute then." She turned to walk away.

"I have your coat," he called, and she stopped. "If your name is Cyn Hargrave. That's the name on the paycheck stub I found in the pocket."

Cyn briefly contemplated telling him to just keep it, but it was the only coat she had, and buying another one, even at thrift-store prices, would put a serious dent in her meager savings. "Yeah, that's me."

"You left it here the other night. I saw it and didn't want anyone else to take it."

"Thanks." She managed a tight smile.

He glanced down at the menu and then held it out to her. "I think I'll have a Reuben. With a Coke."

She wrote down his order and reached for the menu. His fingers brushed hers, and she tried to pull back, but he saw her gold ring. "That's pretty. Reminds me of a ring I helped my brother pick out for a girl he was crazy about. His name was Hunter Vasquez."

As soon as the cop said Hunter's name, Cyn dropped the menu and flat-out ran to the kitchen. *Hunter's brother. He's Hunter's brother, and this is why you've been so freaked out that he's here. It's only a matter of time until he arrests you.*

Hunter had mentioned an older brother once, but she'd never met him and hadn't given him any thought beyond that.

Lenny was hosing down the sink when she burst through the door, and he barely stopped her from running into him. "Everything okay? Marv said you weren't feeling good."

Cyn seized on the excuse. "Yeah. That's right. I thought I was going to barf on my customer out there." She glanced over her shoulder. "I need a big favor, Lenny. He's got my jacket. Do you think you could go get it for me?"

Lenny's face grew angry. "Creeper took your *coat*? That's messed up. Want me to take care of him?"

"No, no. That's okay," Cyn said hastily. "He's a cop."

Lenny nodded and went out to the floor. While she was waiting, Marv came back to the kitchen. "You okay, Cynsation?"

Cyn gave him a weak thumbs-up, but she must have looked pretty bad, because he brought her a bowl of clam chowder and insisted she eat it. She told him what was going on, and he glanced out the window, giving her a play by play.

"Lenny's talking to him now. Looks like the cop is getting up. Bastard better not be skipping out on the check." He shook his fist at the wall.

Cyn's spoon scraped the bottom of the bowl, and she glanced down, surprised that she'd managed to eat it all.

Marv returned to hover over her shoulder. "You want more?" he asked.

"I'm good. Thanks, Marv."

His ears turned red, and he busied himself with something at the sink. "Don't mention it."

The door swung open behind them, and then Lenny came through, holding Cyn's coat triumphantly.

If Cyn was the hugging type, she would have given him one right then. Instead, she gave him a two-finger salute. "I owe you another pack of cigarettes, Lenny."

"No prob— Wait, what do you mean, *another* pack?"

Cyn pulled on her jacket, but she didn't answer him. She had to think. Had to figure out what she was going to do now. "I'm going to cut out early," she said to Marv. "I think I need some more sleep."

He didn't look happy about it, but he agreed. "I expect you on time tomorrow night."

Cyn made a noncommittal noise as she headed for the door. She didn't know if she would be back tomorrow night; it was only a matter of time until the cop arrested her.

"I'm not gonna forget about that 'another pack' comment," Lenny yelled behind her. He pointed to his head. "It's a steel trap up here."

Cyn found herself smiling as she stepped out into the cool morning air. *I might actually miss those guys.*

"Steel trap!" she could still hear him saying. "A goddamn steel trap!"

It wasn't until she was three blocks from her place that she saw the glow of a cigarette in the darkness behind her and realized she was being followed.

CHAPTER SIXTEEN

As soon as Avian came back from following the cop and stepped into Father Montgomery's house he knew something was wrong.

The lights were off, and the house had a cold feeling to it. Empty and barren. Earlier, the priest had told Avian his plans to go make his rounds to visit the sick, which would explain why he wasn't home. But it didn't explain the creeping stillness that hung over the house.

Avian was well acquainted with that feeling. It was death.

Drawing his sword, Avian stalked through the living room to the kitchen. "Father Montgomery? Are you here?"

Father Montgomery's coat was hanging neatly on the rack

by the fireplace, slippers waiting next to the chair he always fell asleep reading in. But Avian didn't smell the lingering odor of the evening coffee Father Montgomery liked to indulge in. The kitchen was just as vacant as the living room.

He moved toward the priest's bedroom next.

The door swung open, revealing a small room with a neatly made bed, an armchair, and a reading table. The sheets were still tucked up under the pillow, not turned down like Father Montgomery always preferred to do right before he went to sleep. He clearly hadn't been there since morning.

Resuming his search, Avian checked the other rooms of the house. They were empty too. Silent as a grave. It wasn't until he went back outside that a faint light from the church caught his eye.

As soon as he took the first step in that direction, he felt the *wrongness* emanating from the building. The pallor of death hung over the gabled roof like a storm squall.

He quickened his pace, and with every step he took, steam rose up from his skin. His horns lengthened. And the scars on his back burned.

It was going to hurt like a son of a bitch to actually step foot inside the church—the demon side of him always reacted most strongly there—but if Father Montgomery was in trouble, then there was no question he was going inside.

A single beam of light spilled feebly onto the ground, as if pointing the way. But Avian could have closed his eyes and kept moving. The darkness trying to pull him back was like a reverse compass. It showed him exactly where it didn't want to go.

Fighting every natural instinct he had, Avian stepped into the church. The light was coming from the pulpit. The pews lining both sides of the room were covered in darkness, and the irony of moving out of the dark and toward the light was not lost on Avian.

A forgotten memory of Father Montgomery trying to teach him the Lord's Prayer rose in his mind, but he would not say it. That prayer was for those who needed it.

Those who needed *Him*.

As the bastard child of two Revenants, Avian had sworn long ago that he would never ask for help. It always came with strings.

The scars on his back—a permanent reminder of his heritage—tightened again, and the ones covering the rest of his body rose to the surface. Breaking through his skin. Burning him from the inside out. Hellfire and damnation rode him hard, screaming for him to turn back. But Avian kept going. Lunging toward that single light.

It was only when a whisper of a psalm reached him and the

shape of a body draped over the pulpit came into view that he staggered to one knee and dropped his weapon.

"Father . . ."

The frail priest was covered in blood, the life force draining out of him with every slow beat of his heart. A trail of droplets showed that he'd been attacked nearby and had tried to crawl to safety, but only made it to the pulpit.

As Avian rushed toward him, he could see the blood on his head and clothes was already stiff. The priest had been lying there for hours.

Gathering him as gently as he could in his arms, Avian flinched when Father Montgomery didn't recognize him.

"Demon," he whispered feebly.

Avian had never thought he had a heart to break. Even after Shelley died right in front of him.

But when he heard that, he knew he was wrong.

Realizing what he must look like, he bowed his head and willed his eye color to change back to brown. It was the least he could give him; the scars and horns wouldn't recede. "Father, I'm sorry I wasn't here."

The priest closed his eyes, and when he opened them again recognition was there. "Avian? My boy . . ." A tear rolled down his cheek. "I didn't think I'd get the chance to say good-bye."

"There's no need for that. This isn't good-bye." Avian smoothed back a wisp of bloodstained hair that lay across Father Montgomery's forehead. "Who did this to you?"

"Yea, though I walk through the valley of the shadow of death, I will fear no evil" were the priest's only words.

"You're not walking through death's valley. I won't let you."

Father Montgomery chuckled, and it turned into a wheeze. "Avian, I haven't told you . . . how proud I am of you. . . ." His eyes widened, and he started coughing.

Avian wiped the blood away from the priest's mouth, but it kept dribbling out like a slow leak of air. "You can tell me tomorrow. As you practice one of your sermons that always turn into a theological debate between us. You'll have lots of time to tell me whatever you want, and I promise to be there for all of it."

"I won't . . ." The light in Father Montgomery's eyes started fading.

"You can't die," Avian demanded. "You *aren't* dying. I can feel when that's about to happen, and I don't feel it with you," he lied.

"A . . . gift," Father Montgomery said slowly. "From our . . . heavenly Father. The gift of . . . peace." He shuddered and then said, "The angels . . . are . . . singing. My . . . favorite Christmas song."

Father Montgomery's favorite song was "O Come, O Come, Emmanuel." It was the only thing he ever requested Avian play for him on the cello.

The crack in Avian's heart deepened. And the black wings that he kept so tightly bound suddenly ripped through his leather jacket and wrapped gently around them.

Taking a final breath, the priest looked up into Avian's eyes. "The angels are beautiful. But none are more beautiful than you."

CHAPTER SEVENTEEN

Cyn ducked behind a Dumpster to try to lose whoever was following her and waited for the footsteps to pass. Her gut instinct told her that it was Declan. She'd seen him with a cigarette that first night in the diner, and he had plenty of reasons to want to question her, since he knew she'd been involved with his brother.

When it sounded like the footsteps had finally passed, Cyn peeked her head out to scan the area. It looked clear. But her wig got snagged on the bottom hinge of the Dumpster door when she tried to stand.

"Son of a bitch," Cyn said under her breath.

Delicately trying to untangle the short black strands, she

almost had it free when Declan's voice came from behind her.

"Need any help?"

Cyn frantically pulled the wig loose and shoved it back onto her head. Smoke drifted past her, and she turned around. "Nope. I got it." She could feel the edges of her forced smile wavering.

"Shouldn't you be back at the diner?" Declan asked, tapping the edge of his cigarette so that the ashes floated to the ground. "I thought you worked the night shift."

"I do. I was just taking a walk."

"Taking a walk." He gave her a hard look. "I thought maybe it was something I said."

He took a step closer, and Cyn willed her legs not to shake. When he glanced down at her ring, she couldn't stop her thumb from rubbing the back of it nervously.

"You know, when they found my brother's mutilated body, I asked if they'd also found a knotted gold ring. I didn't think he'd had the chance to give it to you yet."

Declan brought his cigarette up and held it right next to her cheek. The glowing red end hovered an inch below her left eye, growing brighter and brighter until he suddenly pulled it away.

Cyn flinched, and he laughed. "Guess I was wrong."

The look in his eyes was something Cyn had never seen

before. A chill ran down her spine, and the back of her neck tingled. Why didn't she see the danger in front of her sooner? She'd thought he was just flirting with her, maybe looking for a date.... How could she have been so stupid?

Declan's expression suddenly changed again. The wild look disappeared, and he was nothing more than a charming young man. He dropped the cigarette and then stepped on it. "You should be careful out here all alone, Cyn. You never know what might happen."

Cyn didn't go back to her apartment, just in case Declan was still following her. She didn't know what legal rights he would have to enter the premises, but she didn't want to chance it. As soon as the sun came up, she would return for her stuff. Then it would be time to steal another car and leave town.

She found herself heading toward Father Montgomery's house. She might not be able to tell him *why* she was leaving, but he deserved to know that she wouldn't be coming back. Rubbing her hands over her arms as she walked, Cyn was glad to see the glowing light of the rectory finally come into view.

But it wasn't Father Montgomery's house that had all the lights on. It was the church.

Candelabras lined the pathway leading up to the open

doors, and she could see candles dotting the windowsills inside. It reminded her of a Christmas Eve candlelight ceremony that she went to once when her mother was dating a Methodist.

Wondering why the church was all lit up at four o'clock in the morning, Cyn cautiously stepped inside. A large white shroud covered the pulpit. A shadow caught her eye from the left, and she slipped into the dark recesses of an empty statue alcove, watching as a red-robed figure walked up to the pulpit.

The robed figure pulled back the shroud, and as soon as Cyn saw what was beneath it, she couldn't stop herself from running to him. *"Father Montgomery!"*

Her voice broke as she said his name. With the exception of several dark bruises that marred the side of his face, he could have been sleeping as he lay there.

But Father Montgomery wasn't sleeping. He was dead.

"What did you *do*?" she screamed, launching herself at the robed figure. She began to pummel his chest. The blows didn't seem to faze him, but as her fists made contact, hazy memories of a bar fight came flooding back. She slowly looked up. "You're the guy from the bar. The one who had red eyes and horns and smoke coming off of him. You killed that octopus-arm guy."

His eyes weren't red now, but brown.

She stopped hitting him. He was the one to turn her away

from Father Montgomery's house too, the first time she went to tell him what was happening to her.

"What happened to Father Montgomery?" The church was silent except for the faint echo of her voice. But he refused to answer.

Cyn widened her eyes, pupils dilating, and looked straight at him. "You *will* tell me what happened. You're going to tell me why Father Montgomery is—"

He just crossed his arms and shook his head. "That doesn't work on me."

"Please?" she whispered, leaning forward to put a hand on Father Montgomery's arm. He looked so very much like he was just sleeping and would wake up at any moment. "Please tell me what happened." Tears clouded her vision, and she scrubbed a hand across her face to wipe them away.

"I found him, but I was too late to save him."

She shouldn't have believed him. Not coming across such a strange scene like this. But something deep inside told her he was telling the truth.

The look in his eyes was sorrow.

"What are you going to do with him? I want to help."

"I don't need your help." He gave her a scowl. "Just stay out of my way."

CHAPTER EIGHTEEN

They kept vigil in the church for the rest of the night. Cyn retreated to a pew in the front row and curled up against the hard surface, while Thirteen stayed near the pulpit. She was far enough away from him to stay out of his way, but still close enough to keep watch over Father Montgomery.

She should have been using this time to recite whatever prayers she could remember so that his immortal soul would find comfort in the arms of God. Or something like that. But all she could think about was what he'd said about that squirrel.

I hope there are squirrels in heaven for you, Father Montgomery. I hope you have a nice window with a big backyard and lots of squirrels.

It wasn't a prayer in the traditional sense, but as she closed her eyes and softly said those words, it felt like one to her.

When sunlight started filtering through the windows, Father Montgomery's protector finally rose and left the church. Cyn followed him to the rectory. Her brain felt sluggish. She really needed to get a couple of hours of sleep before she went back for her stuff.

"Can I crash on the couch? I'm beat."

He turned to face her, and she was stunned by his appearance. A slant of sunlight angled across his face and revealed his chiseled cheekbones, a sharp chin, and dark, shoulder-length hair. His eyes were the color of melted chocolate.

Cyn's voice faltered.

He shrugged off the robe and hung it on a coat rack. He was wearing tight black leather pants and a black T-shirt. "And why would you be crashing on the couch?"

"Because I'm tired. I need to get some sleep."

"So go home. Sleep there."

"I can't."

He cocked his head at her, clearly waiting for an explanation. But Cyn wasn't in the mood to give him one.

"Look, I won't bother you, and I won't get in your way. You won't even know I'm here."

"If I want to sit on the couch, you'll be in my way."

Cyn tugged on the back of her wig, and it pulled up high on her forehead. Quickly readjusting it, she said, "Fine. Then I'll sleep in one of the bedrooms, and you can have the couch."

"Not his."

She was *this* close to telling him to go fuck himself. "Are you serious? I just spent the last three hours staring at the body of the only person in this stupid town who's ever tried to help me, and you think I want to *sleep in his bed* while he's growing cold out there? Jesus Christ. I'd rather sleep on the floor."

"Suit yourself." He turned his back to her and went into the kitchen.

Cyn didn't know what to make of that, but she wasn't going to stand here and argue with him about it. The couch it was, then.

At least until he came and forcibly moved her off of it.

The sound of police sirens woke her up, and Cyn panicked. She'd forgotten where she was. Her leg was tangled in a crocheted blanket, and she couldn't get free. When the fog finally lifted and her brain really woke up, she recognized Father Montgomery's house.

Shoving the blanket all the way off, Cyn went to go look

out one of the windows. A bunch of cops were standing around outside the church. Then a stretcher was rolled out and loaded into a nearby van. It was covered with a white sheet.

One of the police officers gestured to the house, and she pulled back from the window. She couldn't go outside while they were there, but she couldn't stay here if any of them decided to come check things out. Cyn glanced at the stairs. There had to be somewhere up there she could hang out while she waited for them to leave.

She went to the attic. It was filled with boxes marked CHURCH CHRISTMAS DECORATIONS and a couple of old pieces of furniture. A large black box shaped like an oversize figure eight was the only thing not covered in dust, and Cyn realized it was some type of musical-instrument case. Obviously well taken care of.

Pulling one of the Christmas boxes over to a small window that overlooked part of the church parking lot, Cyn took a seat. It was a long wait, and she kept dozing off. When she finally heard a door open downstairs and saw that the lot was clear, she went down to the kitchen.

Thirteen was sitting at the table with a cup of coffee in front of him.

"I can make a fresh pot if you want," she offered.

"Do whatever you want. I'm done anyway."

He stood up like he was going to leave. Because of course he was. It wasn't like they were both trying to deal with a murder or anything that just happened.

"Can you just sit with me for, like, five minutes?" Cyn exploded. "I've had a really bad night. Actually, a week of bad nights, and I need—" She stopped and rubbed her temples. A monster headache was forming behind her eyes. "I think I need a drink."

"There's nothing here but cooking sherry. Father Montgomery was old fashioned that way."

"I should have known you would have checked." She moved to a bread keeper on the counter and lifted the lid. Maybe some toast would make her headache go away. "And how can you talk about him so . . . matter of fact like that?"

"Death is pretty matter of fact. You get used to it."

Cyn found the toaster under a cross-stitched appliance cozy and pushed down two pieces of bread. "Death isn't something I ever want to get used to. Death isn't something *most* normal people want to get used to."

She gave him a pointed look so he would know what she was referring to.

"You already know I'm not human, so what is this?"

"What exactly *are* you?" she said bluntly. "With the smoke and the red eyes. Not to mention the horns. . . . Are you the devil?"

He smirked. "The devil. How original. I haven't heard that one in two centuries. I thought this was supposed to be a politically correct day and age."

"Politically correct?" Cyn stared at him in disbelief. "Since when do devil guys worry about being *politically correct*?"

"Since I'm technically a Revenant and *not* the devil, I'd say that falls under the politically correct category. The horns come from my father's side of the family." He crossed his arms, and the action made his T-shirt stretch tightly across his biceps. He saw her gaze shift down. "The burns are another gift from dear old dad. To remember where I came from."

She should have been asking why the burn marks were there before but weren't there now, and why his eyes turned red but didn't stay that way, and if he'd really been around for two centuries, but the word "Revenant" made something twitch in the back of Cyn's brain.

It was familiar. Like she'd heard it before.

Abruptly pushing that thought to the side, Cyn realized that she'd never met someone like him before. Someone who was like her—different. Granted, his case was pretty extreme with the horns and all that, but maybe she could tell him about the faces she'd seen beneath hers.

Maybe he could even help her.

Suddenly, darkness rimmed the edges of her vision and her hearing started to fade. Right before she blacked out, Cyn heard herself groan, "Not now, you son of a bitch."

CHAPTER NINETEEN

S he went down hard and hit the floor with a thud.

"Jesus Christ. She. Just. Won't. Shut. Up."

The voice came out of Cyn, but it wasn't hers. It was a voice Avian hadn't heard in a long time. She pushed herself to a sitting position, her features shifting to reveal another soul trapped inside her body. Just beneath the surface were hints of another face.

A Revenant's face.

"Thirteen? Is it really you?" She grinned up at him.

"Grifyth. It's been a while."

Two hundred years, in fact. Avian kept his distance from the other Revenants most of the time—it wasn't like they were inviting him over for dinner—but every now and then when he ran into someone like Uriel or Acacia, it wasn't all bad. Whenever he ran into Grifyth, though, things went downhill. *Fast.*

His fingers itched to go for his weapon, but he reminded himself that it wasn't just Grifyth he was dealing with. It was still Cyn's body, and her life on the line should the situation escalate.

"I prefer Vincent, actually. You can never find the name Grifyth on any of those mini license plates at the mall." Cyn stood and then grimaced. "Well, this is no fun. All I have is a headache. I thought I hit the ground hard enough to at least get a concussion out of the deal. Fuck."

Avian crossed his arms. "So you're in a girl now. It's a good look for you. You should think about keeping it for a while."

"You have no idea what it's like to be trapped inside such a useless shell," Vincent snarled. "Oh, wait, you do. You're useless too. A Revenant who can't even do his damn job."

"You know that's not my thing. I don't cross Shades over like the rest of you."

Shades were humans who were destined to become guardians of sacred places after their earthly deaths. Graveyards, burial grounds, sanctuaries. But all Shades had a partner they had to find before they could fulfill their duties. Revenants helped them find their other half and then transition to the other side.

Vincent made a sound of disgust. "No, instead you decided to become a babysitter for demons gone rogue. What a waste. You know what I always thought was highly ironic? That the only child of two of the original Revenants turned out to be such a dud. We could have made a sweet team. Your father was pure demon! Imagine the power you could have had." He laughed harshly. "I guess that whole 'sins of the father will be revisited upon the son' thing really bit you in the ass, didn't it?"

"Can't say I have any complaints." Avian gripped the edges of the chair in front of him to stop himself from doing anything stupid. He had rules when it came to humans.

"*Really.* Because I heard the side effects of being only half demon are a bitch. Did you get a tail too? Because I'm pretty sure that's a deal breaker for this one." He pointed at Cyn's body. "Just sayin'."

"Nope. No tail. But I did get the horns."

"Nice! I'll have to find a female Revenant I can screw so maybe one day our bastard child will be as lucky as you."

Avian eased up on the chair and walked over to the fridge. Now he was just getting bored. "Speaking of Revenants . . ." He pulled out a bowl of leftover mashed potatoes and the bottle of ketchup. "You must have fucked something up. I don't think I've *ever* heard of a Revenant being banished inside an Echo." He covered the potatoes with some ketchup. "Do you have to pee sitting down too?"

"Wouldn't know." Vincent's voice had a hard edge to it. "She doesn't let me out that often. I have to fight for the little bit of time I do get."

"Bummer."

"Yeah, but I'm working on getting out permanently. Have you seen my latest artwork?" He rolled up the sleeves of Cyn's shirt. "Fuck. She covered it up."

One by one he ripped the bandages off and then held Cyn's arms out to Avian.

"Used a piece of busted-up floor tile to do it. I aimed for the arteries, of course, but it didn't turn out like I was hoping."

"So you're trying to kill her?"

"Ding, ding, ding! You win a prize. I'm the fifth soul that's been in here. Which means, what, two more *tops* until this body wears out? Who knows how long I'll be trapped until then. I want out, and I want it now."

Avian added more ketchup to his potatoes. "When did this happen? How did you get like this?"

"At a Shade crossover in Sleepy Hollow a couple of months ago. There was supposed to be a new set of Revenants joining the team."

"New Revenants?" The news surprised him. "Uriel and Acacia didn't move on, did they?"

"Nah, those bitches are still here. And they go by Uri and Cacey now." Vincent sat down at the table. "None of us knew who it was going to be until it was over. But I wasn't ready to move on to my after afterlife, if you know what I mean. So I took care of it. Made sure I wasn't the one being forced out of the Revenant gig."

"And I'm guessing that's how *this* happened?" Avian gestured at Cyn's body, and Vincent nodded.

"The other Revenants got pissy with me for interfering and banished me. I ended up here."

"Doesn't seem like their style to pick a human to pay the price for your mistake."

Vincent leaned back in the chair, and the front two legs lifted off the ground. "This body was there the night of the crossover. Guess they got lucky she was an Echo, the perfect place to get rid of me."

Suddenly, Cyn's head jerked to the side.

"Shit. She's coming back," Vincent said. "I'll see you on the flip side, Thirteen. *Good chat.*"

CHAPTER TWENTY

Cyn's body jerked forward, and her head slumped onto the table. It took a minute before she came to. "I need some aspirin," she finally said in a muffled voice. Her face was still planted against the table. "My head hurts."

"They're in the—"

But a loud snore suddenly cut him off. She was asleep. The episode with Vincent must have worn her out.

Avian stood up to return the mashed potatoes and the ketchup to the fridge. Echos were usually stronger than most humans—they had to be, since they were being possessed all the time, but it was hell on their bodies.

And that hell's only going to get worse for her with Vincent in there.

Father Montgomery was right. She needed help, even if she didn't know it yet.

At the thought of Father Montgomery, Avian's chest constricted painfully. Even though all he wanted to do was take the priest's body and go find someplace quiet to lay him to rest, he knew that wouldn't be fair to people like Sister Serena. People who deserved a chance to mourn Father Montgomery's death too.

It was up to him to see that they were notified, so he went to the study to use the phone. An address book was in the top drawer of Father Montgomery's desk, and Avian went right down the list. He kept the conversation brief—repeating only that Father Montgomery had been found deceased in the church.

There was no need for everyone to know the final details of the priest's agonizing death.

When the calls to Father Montgomery's parishioners were finished, he made two more calls. One to the funeral home to tell them he wanted the best casket they had. He didn't care that it was eco-friendly Brazilian cherry wood that had been hand polished by blind monks in Tibet and flown in first class. He also didn't care that it would cost an extra thirty grand to upgrade.

Father Montgomery deserved the best.

The second call he made was to a nearby florist. He bought everything they had in stock, and everything within a twenty-mile radius. The last memory that church would hold wouldn't be of blood, it would be of beauty.

It was almost midnight when he put the phone down, and that was when he found the note. Written in Father Montgomery's familiar handwriting, it was on a sheet of paper that slid out from the back of the address book.

Avian—

I moved your cello from the church to the attic. I hope you don't mind. It's cleaner there, and safer. I know it's been a while since you played, but the next time you come home I was hoping to

The note wasn't finished.

Avian stared down at the words his friend had left behind. His gut churned as he thought about that sense of danger he'd kept experiencing. Why didn't he warn the priest to be more careful? *Why?* The paper wrinkled as his fist closed around it, and his knuckles turned white. Then he smoothed the paper back out and returned it to the address book.

As he stalked out of the study, the attic beckoned him to go up there. Or more so, what was in the attic beckoned him. But Avian ignored the feeling. He hadn't played the cello since Shelley died.

He'd met Shelley because of that cello—she was the store clerk in a dusty little music store, and he was trying to find some replacement strings. They'd started up a conversation, and when it became something more than just friendship between them, he played for her on the nights she had bad dreams. When she couldn't fall asleep.

And when she'd died, he swore to never touch the thing again. Too many memories.

Avian didn't like memories. Avoided making them whenever he could.

He also swore to never get involved with another human again and to keep his distance from Echos. Shelley had been the only good one he'd ever met. Father Montgomery was the exception to his rule about humans, since they'd met long ago. It just wasn't worth the heartache and misery of knowing that, sooner or later, he'd have to watch the mortals he cared for die.

In Shelley's case, it had been sooner.

Avian glanced around Father Montgomery's empty living room. He didn't want to stay here thinking about this anymore.

Cash's bar would serve as a good distraction, and if he got lucky, maybe he'd find an even better distraction—one that involved getting his hands dirty.

The Black Cadillac was busy. Cash had several waitresses in skintight jeans and low-cut tank tops on duty, but as soon as Avian walked in and took a seat in a dark corner Cash could tell something was wrong. He brought over a glass of bourbon right away. "You look like you could use one of these, my friend."

Avian ran a hand over his face. "Is it that obvious?" The smoke-filled room pulsed with an undercurrent of danger that teased the edges of his dark side and forced him to be aware of the tight leash he usually kept it on.

He took the glass, and Cash took a seat. "I found Father Montgomery's body in the church last night."

Cash made the sign of the cross before he caught himself, but Avian waved it off. "What happened?"

"He was murdered." Avian stared down into the bottom of his drink. "It was . . . messy."

"I'm sorry to hear that."

The burn marks on Avian's arms briefly rose up, then faded as his hand tightened on the glass. As much as he'd been hoping to find a good fight here, it was probably in the bar's best interest that he didn't. In this type of mood, there was no telling the amount of damage he could do.

Cash stood. He knew when his friend needed to be alone. "If you need anything, give a shout. The bar, a bottle, anything." He offered his hand and Avian took it.

"Thanks." Avian drained the last of his drink and then stood up too. "Think I'm just going to hit the road. Take a drive and clear my head."

Returning to the register, Cash watched him leave, knowing full well that he wasn't just going for a drive. Thirteen was already on the hunt. He wouldn't stop until he found whoever had killed that priest.

And he *would* find out.

He always did.

On his way out of town, Avian passed Pete's Salvage Yard and made a last-minute decision to stop. Letting the bike idle, he put two fingers to his lips and whistled.

The hellhound that guarded the junkyard immediately came running and leapt straight up and over, clearing the ten-foot-tall gates with ease. His eyes burned red as he pranced from foot to foot with nervous energy, and a whine rose from his throat.

Avian's eyes turned red to match, and he felt his horns lengthen. "Ready to hunt?" he asked.

The hellhound's ears lay back, and his spine went rigid. Avian revved the motorcycle and then spun out, circling around the gravel driveway before pulling onto the main road. The hellhound kept up with him every step of the way.

Avian buried the needle on the bike's speedometer and roared down the highway. The hellhound was a blur beside him, all lean muscle and quivering flesh. He reached out a hand to touch the beast, and steam rose from the hellhound's fur, curling around his fingertips.

A flash of searing heat blasted through him. Misery and suffering melted holes in his brain so intense, it made his eyeballs ache in their sockets. The burn marks on his back and shoulders rose to the surface in response, breaking through the skin.

It was a memory from hell. A flashback of what it felt like to be down there.

Probably something the beast had already forgotten if he'd been topside long enough, but the demon side of Avian had memories from that place too—he'd been born there. Every day, he felt that pull to find a way to see just how much it really felt like home.

He rode for another hour before he stopped for gas. As soon

as he pulled into the empty station the hellhound went on high alert, heading for the back of the building. Avian followed him around to a dark parking lot and saw two people huddled over a body. Faint slurping sounds let him know that this was the kind of fight he was looking for—vampires.

"Good dog," he said, drawing the blade from his jacket.

Since the hellhound's purpose was to protect consecrated ground, he recognized the scent of death. And that included the undead.

Avian moved his head from side to side, cracking his neck as he slowly advanced. Neither of the vampires looked up until he was practically on top of them. When they finally did raise their faces, they had bull-like heads and long, forked tongues. More members of the Navarro coven.

Damn, these guys get around.

Whistling again for the hellhound, Avian said, "Hey, pup, what do you say I take the ugly one, and you take the . . . Oh, hell, they're both ugly fuckers. I'll just take the one on the right and you get the one on the left."

Apparently the hellhound agreed, because his jaws were already wide open, and he leapt at the throat of the vampire on the left, tearing into him with a blood-spurting frenzy that Avian matched with his weapon slash for slash.

Chapter Twenty-One

Cyn woke up to a stiff neck and a raging headache. The last thing she remembered was talking to Thirteen. She glanced down, realizing that she'd fallen asleep at Father Montgomery's kitchen table. The weariness that came along whenever the darkness took over sucked all the energy out of her.

A sound came from outside, and a light over the small shed in the backyard illuminated the outline of someone pushing a motorcycle into it. A couple of minutes later, Thirteen came inside the house. His hands were covered with little black spots, and a clump of something dark and brown stained his left cheek. He went directly to the sink and started washing up.

Oil. It's just oil from his bike.

Finally, he said without looking up, "You're still here?"

"I guess I was just on my way out."

"Well, don't let me stop you." He dried his hands and then reached into the cabinet to his left and pulled out an empty glass.

A glass of water and some headache medicine sounded heavenly right about now. So Cyn said, "Can I get one of those?"

He left the cabinet door open instead of getting her a cup and walked away from it. Cyn gritted her teeth and moved slowly toward the sink, fighting the tiredness that threatened to consume her. Everything ached. Her back, her hips, even her knees.

Her fingers trembled as she filled the glass, and when she looked down, she saw that her shirt sleeves were rolled up. Exposing her arms and exposing her wounds. The bandages were missing.

Cyn stopped cold. "Did you do this to me?"

"Cut you? No."

"I know you didn't cut me. I meant, did you take off my bandages?"

"That was all you."

"For some reason I decided to just take them off? Why the fuck would I do that?"

"You had your reasons." He walked over to the door and held it wide open. "Now, you said something about leaving?"

"Yeah. Right." Cyn shook her head in disbelief and dropped her glass on the counter. She'd actually thought he might be able to help her. *So much for that.* Carefully rolling down the sleeves of her shirt, Cyn doubled back into the living room and found her coat lying on the floor beside the couch, then she met him at the door. Her breath fogged up, and the cold night air bit right through her. *Damn, it's cold out.*

"The funeral will be at the church," he said.

"Yeah, okay."

Cyn turned her back before she could say anything more. Before she could beg him to let her stay a little longer inside the warm house, before she could tell him how even sleeping on a lumpy couch was ten times better than sleeping on a concrete floor, before she could ask if he'd give her a ride back so she wouldn't have to walk in the cold, before she could say that she didn't know if Hunter's brother would be waiting for her when she got back to her apartment and that she really, really, really just wanted someone to be there in case he was.

He didn't want to hear any of those things, and she didn't want to have to say them.

He caught up with her about ten minutes after she'd left.

Cyn heard a motorcycle behind her as she walked away from Father Montgomery's house, hands stuffed deep into her pockets to keep them warm. She grimaced when she saw the black-clad rider. "Keep driving, keep driving, keep driving."

He cut her off by stopping the bike right in front of her.

Cyn tried to go around him, but he just straddled the bike and slowly followed her. She let it go on for a few minutes before coming to a halt. "What? Why are you here?"

"To give you a ride back to your place."

"*Now* you suddenly want to give me a ride? Why not when I left the house?"

He didn't answer, and she started to walk again. "Okay, come on," he said. "It's nighttime and I felt bad, all right? Anything could happen to you out here, and I don't need that on my conscience."

"I'm fine, and your conscience is clear. I absolve you. Now go away."

She faced the wind again and put her head down. The slow squeak of a rolling wheel became her constant companion as she resumed her pace. And it was *insanely* annoying.

"I could do this all night," he said. "But's going to take a lot longer this way."

"Nope." Cyn shook her head. "I don't do motorcycles." She learned that the hard way when she stole one once and wiped out on a dirt road. The jagged scar zigzagging up her left knee didn't let her forget it.

"I'm not asking."

"Well, I'm not riding." She pulled down on the back of her wig.

"Fine. Have it your way. But it's a long walk."

"How do you know? Maybe it's only a short walk. Maybe I like the fresh air."

"You like it so much, your lips are turning blue? And I know where you live because I took you home from the bar."

Cyn turned to face him. "That was you?"

"Yeah. Now get on."

Cyn glanced around. She hadn't seen any cars yet, and it might be a while until one came by. And even then, in order for her to take it, the conditions had to be just right. She wasn't going to leave kids standing out in the cold.

She was about to turn him down again, but then he did something that threw her for a loop—he smiled.

A really, really great smile.

It was actually more of a side grin, but it made Cyn feel a rush of nerves and sweaty palms and the sudden urge to check her teeth and make sure nothing was stuck in them.

Taking a step back, she tried not to notice how his dark hair brushed the edges of his jacket. Just how she liked it— long enough to run her fingers through. Shadows played up his angular jawline, giving him cheekbones to die for and lips that would make a model jealous.

Her gaze fell lower, taking in his long, lean body, and she took note of the fact that he had to be at least six foot four. The perfect height for her. If she moved close enough, she'd fall in line right with his chest. Her head would be able to tuck under his.

Keep walking by yourself out here in the cold, or get on the back of a hot guy's bike and wrap your arms around him? No brainer, Cyn.

"Yeah, um . . . I . . . yeah." She climbed behind him, holding tightly to his waist as soon as she was situated. His motorcycle was ancient. It looked like it could fall apart at the first pothole. "Is this thing safe?" she yelled into his ear as he cranked the engine. "It looks . . . old."

"This is a Vincent Black Lightning. Of course it's safe. Fast, too. Haven't you heard of Rollie Free? Riding across the

Bonneville Salt Flats in Utah on a Black Lightning?" His voice was incredulous. "He took the world land speed record in 1948."

"Sorry. My neighbor keeps stealing my copy of *Motorcycle Weekly*." They drove back onto the road and started picking up speed. "No helmets?" she yelled into his ear again.

"Sorry. My neighbor keeps stealing all my helmets."

Cyn bit back a grin and buried her face in his jacket. The wind rushing past her ears was cold. The back of her wig started to take flight, and she freed up one hand, using it to clamp down on top of her head. After a while, her ears and cheeks grew numb, and she actually started to enjoy the feeling of freedom.

Not enough to make motorcycle riding in October a habit or anything—but she was glad when, twenty minutes later, they came to her building.

As they drove up to the door Cyn kept an eye out for Declan. She didn't see him, but she wasn't going to take any chances. "Could you hang around for, like, five minutes? Let me know if anyone comes?"

"Expecting company?"

"Something like that."

"Five minutes."

"Thanks." She got off his bike and glanced around again before going inside.

Crossing over to her suitcase, Cyn began stuffing clothes into it. "Ready to find a new place, guys?" She talked to her plants as she worked. "I'm tired of the cold. What do you say we head south. Someplace warm. Maybe Mexico."

She went into the bathroom to gather her toothbrush but stopped when she saw the toilet. The knife was still inside the water tank.

"Just leave it," she said out loud. "Forget about it."

What if someone finds it and connects you to it? Do you really want to give them evidence to pin something else on you? Take it. It might not be such a bad thing to have a weapon to protect yourself.

Cyn fished the knife out of the tank and then wrapped it in an old towel. Burying it in the very bottom of her suitcase, she zippered the bag up and hauled it over to her sleeping bag, which rolled up like a cinnamon bun and fit snugly on top.

The last thing she did was retrieve her battered copy of *The Bell Jar* from beneath the three-legged table. Not only was it an excellent stabilizer, but it also served the dual purpose of holding all the cash she'd managed to save up over the last two months. The inside pages had been hollowed out.

But when she opened it, there wasn't a stack of tens and twenties waiting for her. There wasn't any money at all. The only thing inside the book was another one of Declan's business cards.

This time it had TRY TO RUN NOW written on the back of it.

CHAPTER TWENTY-TWO

S hit, shit, *shiiiiiiit!*" Cyn yelled, ripping the card up and throwing the pieces onto the concrete floor. All of the money she'd so painstakingly saved up week after begrudging week was gone. Twelve hundred dollars. Completely gone. "You fucking asshole!" she screamed.

Declan had hit her where it hurt.

It wasn't like she could go to the police. They'd lock her behind bars for what happened in Sleepy Hollow first, and ask questions later.

The door behind her opened, and Avian came in. "Everything okay?"

"Oh, yeah, everything's fine." She tugged at the back of her wig and paced. "My life is completely fucked, but hey, it's fine."

He glanced around the room. "Are you going to tell me what just made you lose your shit?"

Cyn continued to pace. "My money's gone, Hunter's brother is stalking me, and now . . ." She shook her head. "Forget it. Just forget I said anything."

"Who's Hunter? And why is his brother stalking you?"

"Hunter is my— He was my— Just someone I knew."

"And money is the other problem?"

At her nod, Avian pulled out his wallet and took out a fifty-dollar bill. "Here. Take it."

Cyn ignored him.

He came closer and jammed the money into the front of her jacket. "Don't say I never gave you anything. Your five minutes is up—I'm out of here."

Cyn glared at him as he walked away. She realized that if she didn't take his money, she literally had nothing, but it annoyed the *shit* out of her that he could be so nonchalant about it.

"Thanks," she said begrudgingly as he headed out the door.

He didn't respond.

Cyn sighed, listening to his motorcycle start up. It wasn't like she wanted him to stay, and be her knight in shining armor or anything. But damn. Just leaving her here like this?

She didn't know *what* to do. Even if she managed to find another car to steal, between gas and food, fifty bucks wasn't enough to get her very far. No matter how careful she was. Of course, there *was* the option of using her mind mojo to get her across the state. She could will someone else to pay for all the gas and food. *Hell, maybe even get a hotel along the way. . . .*

Cyn shook her head. Taking a car for a joyride and making people leave her big tips was as far as she was willing to go. She still had principles.

So, what do you do now, genius?

Cyn resumed her pacing. She thought up several new plans and discarded each one just as quickly as it came, for hours. The only thing she knew for sure was that in order to leave town she needed a way to come up with more money.

She also knew that it wasn't safe to stay here anymore.

"I can get another wait job," she mused to herself. "Find a different diner, change my name, get a new wig. No . . . I'll dye my hair this time. Maybe even cut it. . . ."

Right now, though, she needed another place to stay. And there was really only one option: Father Montgomery's house. He had a spare bedroom, and as long as she steered clear of Thirteen there was no reason why she couldn't stay there. Father

Montgomery *had* told her that he was there to help if she needed anything.

She was just belatedly taking him up on that offer.

Cyn used the fifty bucks to call for a cab and crammed her suitcase and all of her plants into the backseat with her, then had the driver make a quick stop at the liquor store along the way.

If this was going to work, she was going to have to bribe the beast.

Chapter Twenty-Three

When the doorbell at Father Montgomery's house rang, Avian answered it with a scowl on his face and a sword in his hand. It was a shitty time for visitors. He'd been right in the middle of stripping the oil off his blade.

"Um, hi?" Cyn was standing there juggling her plants and a couple of brown bags. "What are you doing?"

"Cleaning my sword. What does it look like I'm doing?" He gestured to the cloth draped over his shoulder, and then behind him to the supplies spread across the kitchen table.

"It looks to me like you're answering the door with a very sharp, probably very illegal weapon. Like a crazy person. Who does that?"

"Someone who was interrupted while cleaning their weapon does that. Why else would I—" He stopped and then lowered the sword. "Why am I arguing about this with you? Why are you here again?"

"I need ten bucks for the cab ride. The fifty wasn't enough."

He raised an eyebrow.

She dropped several of the plants and then held out one of the brown bags. "I brought you Buffalo Trace. That's what you were drinking at the bar, right?" She glanced down. "Also Jack Daniels, Jim Beam, and Russian vodka."

He still didn't say anything. Maybe she'd go away if he just ignored her.

"Seriously, the cab driver needs ten bucks. And you know I don't have it, so put down the sword and pay up. He's not going anywhere, and I don't think he'll accept alcohol as payment."

As if on cue, the cab driver angrily honked his horn.

Reluctantly propping his sword up by the door, Avian took the brown bag and sat it on the floor. Then he took a step outside and ran into Cyn's suitcase.

"Sorry," she called, moving into the house. "My bad."

He never liked that phrase. *My bad.* Why did modern-day slang have to sound so stupid?

The cabbie gave another angry honk.

I should have brought the sword.

Shoving a hand into his back pocket, Avian reached for his wallet and fished out a twenty. At least this way he could make one of them go away. After he had some bourbon, he'd call for a different cab driver to come back for *her.*

Avian's face was enough to make the driver's hand shake as he rolled down the window just enough to take the money. "Change?" he mumbled.

"Keep it," Avian growled.

The cab driver didn't have to be told twice. He pulled away in such a hurry, he spewed gravel from the loose stone driveway.

When Avian turned back to the house, Cyn was rolling her suitcase up the steps. He took the stairs in two strides and found her putting her plants in the window over the sink. She was just making herself right at home.

"What do you think you're doing?"

"I need a place to stay. Father Montgomery offered me his help if I ever needed it, and right now I need it."

"Does this have anything to do with what happened earlier?"

"Yeah. I told you. My money's all gone. I have nothing."

"Why don't you go to the cops? File a report and let them know you were robbed."

Avian didn't miss the brief flash of panic in her eyes at the word "cops."

"I can't."

"Can't? Or won't?"

"Either. Take your pick." She turned around to face him but looked down at her feet as she spoke. It was obviously a struggle to admit she needed help. "I won't stay long. Trust me, I don't want to be here any more than you want me here. I just . . . don't have anywhere else to go. Nowhere that's safe."

Avian crossed his arms. She could have used her influence as an Echo and made someone else give her a place to stay. She'd tried with Cash in the bar to get another drink, and with him in the church to tell her what happened to Father Montgomery. Clearly, she knew what she was capable of.

Yet she'd come here. And didn't try to use her influence on him again.

A begrudging respect filled him. But she was still an Echo, and she could still prove to turn out as bad as the rest of them. He'd sworn never to get involved with any of them again, and that included helping them out. As far as he was concerned, Echos were on their own.

So why was he actually considering letting her stay?

To keep an eye on her. No telling what else Vincent has planned.

"Pick any room except for his," he heard himself saying. "And you can stay."

She gave him a look of disbelief. "What?"

"You heard me." He rifled through the brown bags until he found the one that held the bourbon and pulled it out.

"No strings attached? You're not going to do anything weird, are you? Like murder me in my sleep?"

"Of course not. I have rules when it comes to humans."

"What's that supposed to mean?"

"I stick strictly to the supernatural." He left out the part about how technically this included her since she was an Echo. "I don't mess with humans, and they don't mess with me."

Her skeptical look turned to relief. "Okay. Fine. Glad to hear it. I'm not going to argue with that." She turned back to the sink and watered her plants, then grabbed two glasses. "What should we start with first?"

Avian brought the bottle of bourbon to his lips and took a swallow. "*We?* I thought this was payment for me letting you stay here."

"You thought *all* of this was payment?" Cyn cleared a spot at the table and sat down. "Um, no." Pouring some whiskey into her glass, she lifted it high. "To Father Montgomery."

Avian clinked his bottle against her glass. "To Father Montgomery."

She finished her drink in one shot and refilled it. "He told me about you, you know. Said he helped someone with a bad attitude. His church didn't want him to, but he did anyway."

"*Bad attitude?* He said that?"

"Okay, I'm paraphrasing. He didn't exactly say the words "bad attitude." I'm sure it was just something like you had trust issues. Which, hey, who doesn't?" She drained her glass. "You have to admit, though, everything about you kind of screams 'bad attitude.'"

Avian shrugged. "It usually works in my favor. People learn to stay away."

"'People,' right. And by that you mean humans."

He tipped his bottle at her in a you-got-it gesture.

"But not me."

"Not you." He gave her a long look. "Why is that?"

"I don't know, actually. I think it's because of whatever's inside of me. I'm pretty messed up in a big way."

Surprise hit Avian. *So she knows she's an Echo?*

Cyn rubbed her thumb along the edge of her glass. "Ever since I was a little kid, I've had these, like . . . hallucinations or something. This feeling of darkness that comes over me. And then I see faces. Beneath my face. Only one at a time, and they come and go. It's like people are living under my skin." She gave a harsh laugh. "Do you have any idea what that's like when you're seven years old? To tell someone that when you look into a mirror, your face isn't your own?"

She was lost in a memory. He could see it in the faraway look in her eyes.

"None of them could ever see it," Cyn said softly. "Only me."

Her grip tightened on the glass, and then she suddenly shook her head. Glancing up with a dazed expression, she reached for the bottle of whiskey. "What was I saying?"

"That you don't stay away from me because you're messed up," Avian supplied.

"Right." She unscrewed the cap and covered the bottom of her tumbler with more amber liquid. "I'm messed up. What about you? You said you're a Remnant. What's that all about? See any weird visions or hallucinations, like me?"

He grimaced. "I'm a Revenant. Complicated story. Although it's what I am, not who I am. And no. No visions or hallucinations."

Cyn toasted him. "I like that. It's not *what* you are, it's *who* you are that counts. I'm Cyn, and you're Thirteen." Then she frowned. "What kind of a name is that?"

"The kind given to you by those who don't think you deserve a real one."

"Maybe they called you that because it's tattooed on your neck."

Avian's fingers tightened around the bourbon bottle he still held. He hadn't touched it beyond that first sip. "That's just a reminder I'm a mistake that never should have happened."

"I know a lot about mistakes."

She was just about to pour herself another refill when he reached out and took the whiskey from her. "That's enough for now. It won't solve any of your problems."

"I've only had one glass," she protested. "Two at the most."

"No, you haven't."

"Yes, I have."

He held up the half-empty bottle. "This says you've had a lot more."

"I did *not* drink all of that," Cyn said indignantly. "You had some."

He gave a pointed look at the still-full bottle of bourbon in his other hand.

"All right, all right." She rolled her eyes and stood up. "I guess that's enough for now." Putting the cap back on the bottle of Jack, she placed it with the rest of the alcohol and then said, "But you're a real buzz kill, you know that?"

Chapter Twenty-Four

An urgent craving for nicotine hit Cyn around three a.m. She was on Father Montgomery's couch again, flipping through late-night infomercials on an old TV that looked like it had been there since the sixties. She tried to ignore the feeling, but the need for a cigarette was killer and she finally gave in.

She didn't see Avian as she tiptoed through the house, and assumed he was sleeping. After he'd cut her off, he'd gone back to cleaning his sword and she'd claimed the couch. That was where the only TV in the house was. She didn't see the keys to Father Montgomery's twenty-year-old sedan either but got lucky when she rummaged through the coat pocket of the jacket he still had hanging by the front door and found them there.

Twenty minutes down the road, an open gas station came into sight, and she pulled in, leaving the car idling. Cyn didn't like what she was about to do, but she was desperate.

Strolling casually into the store, she took in the lay of the land. The night clerk was bent down beneath the counter, and she couldn't tell if it was a man or a woman. Hopefully, it would be a man. For some reason, her mind mojo always worked better on men.

Cyn glanced bemusedly at a motorcycle magazine on the rack to her left and even briefly flipped through it while keeping an eye on the counter. When the clerk finally stood up again, Cyn saw that he was a tall man in his thirties, wearing a green and yellow uniform. His face lit up when he saw her.

Jackpot.

She put the magazine down and made her way over to him. Eyes wide, pupils dilating, she leaned across the counter. "I need you to get me a pack of Virginia Slims." Her stomach growled loudly, and she glanced down at the snacks. "And these"—she reached for the first thing there—"pistachios, please."

He grinned happily and turned around to get the cigarettes. When he turned back to give them to her, he said something, but no sound came out of his mouth.

"What's that?" Cyn leaned in closer.

He spoke again—she *saw* his mouth move—but there wasn't any sound. And then Cyn realized that she couldn't hear anything else around her either. Not the radio that had been blaring, not the buzz of beer coolers, and not the idling engine of the car outside.

Everything was completely muffled, and then her vision went black.

Cyn woke up behind the counter. A lit cigarette in one hand and a loaded gun in the other.

Pure terror came over her, and she carefully set the gun down on the floor and moved away from it. She threw the cigarette onto the floor too and crushed it beneath the palm of her hand. Not even registering the sting as it burned into her flesh.

Cyn's entire body shook as she thought about what might have happened while she blacked out. Did she hurt someone else? Or was she just going to hurt herself?

Getting to her feet, Cyn walked the empty store, looking for the night clerk. "Hello?" she called. "Anyone here?" The cash register appeared to be untouched, and nothing was broken or obviously missing. But he was nowhere to be found.

Then she glanced outside and saw that Father Montgomery's car was gone. *Did he take it? Did I tell him to take it?*

She didn't trust herself. She needed help.

Her gaze fell on a phonebook sitting on top of the counter, and she flipped through it, praying that the number for Father Montgomery's church would be listed there.

It was. And so was the rectory.

She dialed the rectory number and waited anxiously as every ring went by. It took ten tries, but she kept calling, and eventually a male voice picked up.

"What?"

"It's Cyn. I need your help. I'm at the gas station right down the road. Something . . . bad happened."

"I'll be right there."

He hung up before she had a chance to say anything else. As she waited, she sat on the floor and lit up another cigarette. Staring at the gun the whole time.

He came stalking through the door five minutes later and found her there.

"Are you okay? What happened?" His eyes were brown with a hint of red around the edges.

"I don't know. I borrowed Father Montgomery's car because I needed a pack of cigarettes. But the car's gone now, and so is the clerk. I don't know what happened. There's a gun, and I don't know how I got it or where it came from."

Her head was beginning to hurt, and she rubbed the back of her neck. "I think I blacked out," she babbled on. "I don't know what's happening to me."

Cyn stared up at him and felt like her soul was being laid bare. Could he see the darkness inside her? Did he know about the money she'd influenced people to give her, the cars she'd stolen, and what she'd done to Hunter?

"I can read your memories," he said. " It should help us figure out what happened here."

He slanted his head, and a piece of brown hair fell across his face. He ran a hand through his hair, raking it back, and it suddenly struck Cyn how very human that gesture was. She nodded her consent, and he touched her forehead. He closed his eyes for a couple of minutes, and then it was all over.

"You told the clerk to take the car and he did. Then you went behind the register, smoked a cigarette, and found the gun under the counter. Then you woke up."

"That's it?" Astonishment filled Cyn's voice. "That's all that happened?"

"That's it."

He left out the part where Vincent had wanted to turn the gun on her. To follow through with his exit plan. If she hadn't come to when she did, she probably wouldn't still be alive.

"But what about the surveillance videos? They're going to see all of this, and even if I didn't technically do anything wrong, the cops are still going to come asking questions."

Avian glanced up at the small white camera propped above them. "No blinking light. For confirmation, he pulled it down and looked it over before putting it back. "It's a fake."

Relief swept over Cyn as he checked the other three cameras in the opposite corners of the store and confirmed they were fakes too.

When Avian came back to the register, he walked around the counter and picked up the gun, carefully wiping it clean of any prints with the edge of his T-shirt. Then he returned it to its spot under the counter. He also wiped down the phone she used.

Everything looked the same way it had when she first walked in—minus the store clerk.

"Let's go," Avian said.

"We can't leave the store with no one in it."

In reply, he flipped the light switch off, turned the OPEN sign to CLOSED on the door, and locked the door behind them. "Done."

Cyn followed him out to his motorcycle and glanced one more time at the now-darkened store. She still felt edgy and nervous. Without another word, they climbed onto the back of his bike and he drove away.

But they didn't go back to the church. He just kept driving right past the rectory and ended up on a road Cyn didn't recognize. She closed her eyes and leaned into him, breathing in the cold night air. It was a jagged knife to her lungs that kept her alert and awake. A shock to her system. Like finding yourself suddenly swimming in a cold pool.

Or maybe it was more like drowning.

The road turned into a wooded lane, and trees crowded around them. She could see that less than a hundred feet ahead the path dead-ended and there was nothing but a yawning black hole. Then Cyn realized that the distant roaring and crashing noises she could hear were coming from the black hole. As the bike got closer, the noises got louder.

He took them right up to the edge and parked.

It was a bluff overlooking a massive waterfall. Moonlight revealed white-crested currents crashing against giant boulders at the bottom of the falls, and even from as high up as she was, Cyn could feel the magnetic pull of the water coursing through her.

She glanced over at Avian. "Thought you might want some time to think," he said.

"Yeah. Thanks." She put her hands in her pockets and felt the pack of cigarettes. "Do you mind if I smoke?"

He shook his head. Cyn pulled one out but didn't light it right away. Her thumb stroked the smooth packet as she thought everything over. *What if the next blackout is the one where I hurt someone? Or kill them? Again. I can't let that happen. I have to stop this.*

Bracing herself, she took a step forward.

Thirteen's hand shot out and gripped her shoulder. "Don't get any ideas. At least not while I'm here. I don't want to have to clean up the mess."

"It's not safe for anyone to be around me anymore. It's not safe for *me* to be around me anymore. This is the only way to make sure I don't hurt someone again—"

She stopped. Realizing what she'd just said.

"Stop being so dramatic. You're an Echo. That's the reason for the blackouts."

His words stopped her dead in her tracks.

"I'm a . . . what?"

"An Echo. A conduit for souls of the dead. That's why you can't remember anything during the blackouts. There's another soul inside you that comes to the surface during that time."

"Wait . . . so you're saying I have someone else inside me?" Her voice grew shrill. "I *knew* it! I knew I was possessed."

"It's not possession. That happens when someone is sharing their body with a demonic entity. You share yours with the dead. Misplaced souls."

"So that means I have *two* souls? How is that even possible?"

"Technically, your soul is made up of other people's souls. It's complicated, but the basic gist is that when certain people die, their souls seek out an Echo to live in for a while before finally moving on. I don't know if it's some unfinished-business shit or what, but that's what happens. They have to go somewhere. When they're finally ready to move on to the afterlife, a little piece of them gets left behind and becomes part of your soul."

"Like a quilt." Cyn turned to face him. "My soul is made up of a bunch of other pieces of souls like the squares of fabric that make a quilt."

"Right. So *your* soul is a quilt. Get it? Got it? Good."

"How long does someone else get to live inside my body?"

"Until they move on or another soul takes over. You said you see faces in the mirror beneath yours. Are they continuously there?"

Cyn shook her head. "Sometimes there's a break. Every time that's happened, I thought I was fixed. I should have known better. It always came back." Cyn glanced up at him. "Why did this happen to me?"

"I don't know." He shrugged. "It's who you are. You just have to deal with it."

"Just *deal* with it? Do you have any idea what it feels like to lose complete control over your body? To wake up and have no idea where you are or what you've been doing? To be the freak on the playground who scratches her face because she's trying to get rid of the man she sees there every time she looks in the mirror?"

Cyn stopped abruptly and took a step away from him. But Avian reached for her. Wrapping his fingers around her arm.

"I know what it's like to be fucked up. You're not the only one. To know that you're a mistake you can't do anything about. I know what it's like to be despised by everyone you know, to do things that you wish you could take back. . . ."

"Like what?" Cyn taunted. She was angry at him. Angry at this piece of information he just dropped in her lap. Angry that he could act like it was no big deal. "What do you wish you could take back?"

His gaze shifted down to her lips. "This. I know I'm going to want to take back this."

And then he kissed her.

CHAPTER TWENTY-FIVE

She tasted like the rain. Cold and clean and fresh. Her fists wrapped around his shirt, and she pulled him closer, making a soft sound. Her lips were cool, but the fire inside him burned hot. His hand slid from her wrist up to her cheek. His thumb tracing a path against her skin.

There hadn't been anyone else since Shelley died. He'd never even been tempted. Until now.

Then she pushed him away.

"Can you take me back to the house? I just want to go back."

She turned away from him, and he saw it for the rejection that it was.

Avian nodded, and she silently climbed onto the motorcycle.

She was so slight, he could barely feel her behind him. When they finally pulled up to the rectory, she left him outside without a second glance and went into the house. He put his motorcycle away and then followed her.

She was on the couch when he walked in, flipping idly through the pages of *Through the Looking Glass, and What Alice Found There*. She frowned every now and then as she read.

Ten minutes later, she put the book down and disappeared from the room. The sound of a shower started. When she came back, her hair was blond instead of brown, and her skin was slightly damp. She smelled like something fruity.

Avian was trying to figure out if the smell was bubble gum or cherry, then suddenly realized what he was doing. He left the room abruptly.

His bike needed some attention. Outside, away from here.

Away from *her*.

After a couple of hours, Avian called it quits on the bike and went back inside the house to wash the grease from his knuckles. Cyn had fallen asleep on the couch. A tangle of blond hair was crumpled on the cushion next to her.

A wig.

That explained the sudden change in hair color right after her shower.

Her bare neck was exposed, and something caught his eye. He moved closer. Belatedly registering the fact that her real hair color was the exact same shade of red as Shelley's, he stared down at the three freckles on the back of her neck forming a perfect triangle.

It was the same spot where Shelley had gotten her tattoo: three dots to make a triangle.

Three dots. Three freckles.

It was a perfect match.

She suddenly rolled over, and he took a step back. Not wanting to look like a . . . well, like a creepy guy who was going to murder her in her sleep like she thought.

"'One, two! One, two!'" she mumbled. "'And through and through. The vorpal blade went snicker-snack!' Snicker-snack. Snicker-snack. The blade went snicker-snack!"

He bent to pick up the book she'd been reading. That was something from the poem "Jabberwocky."

Cyn rolled over again and tossed one arm above her head. Making little whimpering sounds. Like she was lost. Or scared. "They can't get me. Don't let them get me!"

He went over to her, shaking her shoulder. "Cyn. Wake up. You're having a night—"

As soon as he touched her, garbled flashes of police sirens, bloodstained sheets, and the sound of her crying instantly filled his head. It was obvious that something bad had happened.

The question was what.

Avian was so focused on deciphering between what was real and what was just a dream that he didn't realize he was still shaking her.

"What are you *doing*?"

Cyn's voice immediately broke his concentration.

She pulled away from him and sat up. Tucking her knees against her chest, she sank back into the couch. The look on her face was fear.

Was she was afraid of *him*? "You were having a nightmare. I was just trying to wake you up."

"I have a hard time sleeping sometimes. Just leave me alone."

"Fine with me," he said, turning to leave the room. He didn't stay where he wasn't wanted. "Next time I won't try to help."

CHAPTER TWENTY-SIX

Cyn's hands were shaky as she sat up on the couch and massaged her temples. She'd been dreaming about something when Thirteen had woken her up, but she couldn't remember what. Now she just felt strung out and even more exhausted. Like she hadn't gotten any sleep at all.

She was hungry, too. When she walked into the kitchen, she saw Father Montgomery's car back in the driveway and the keys sitting on the counter. How Thirteen had managed that she didn't know. But she wasn't going to stick around to ask.

I'll go get something to eat at the diner. Marv will spot me a meal.

There were a handful of cars in the diner parking lot when she pulled in, but she didn't see Marv's beat-up blue pickup truck in its familiar spot. Lenny's vintage Camaro was there, though. She glanced through the front windows to see if Declan was inside, but couldn't see the table in the back where he liked to sit.

Go in through the kitchen. Even if he's there, you should be able to avoid him.

Cyn went in and found Lenny bent over the disposal in the sink. "Is it stopped up again?" she asked, leaning against the doorway.

"Another damn spoon." His arm was buried up to his elbow, but he gave a grunt and then grinned. "Got it!"

Tossing the mangled piece of silverware into the box by the back door, he shook his head. "Don't know why Marv insists on using nice silverware. The customers aren't coming for his place settings. He could use plastic forks for all they'd care. So, where the hell have you been?"

"Sick." Cyn shrugged and moved to the griddle. Pancakes were ordered so often that they kept a jug of premixed batter next to it, ready to go at all times. The griddle sizzled and spit as she poured several dime-size pancakes.

Lenny washed his hands. "Does this mean you're feeling

better? Dougie Ray's been covering your shift, and he ain't happy about it. Marv's not happy about it either."

"Not sure yet." Cyn flipped the pancakes onto a plate and took a seat at the small table. She was so hungry she was done with her meal in three minutes flat. Gathering the dirty dishes, she deposited them in the sink and impulsively gave Lenny a kiss on the cheek. "Don't say anything to Marv about me being here, okay, Lenny?"

"Okay, but if you don't hightail it out of here, he's gonna find out anyway." Lenny gestured to the open back door. "He's parking right now."

"I'll go out the front." Cyn gave him a salute and a grin. "And remember, I was never here."

"Yeah, yeah." Lenny muttered, returning to the griddle. "I heard you the first time." But he returned her grin.

Cyn was so busy watching for Marv that as she made her way out onto the floor she forgot to look at the customers.

They got a good look at her, though. Or, at least, one of them did.

She froze in place when she heard Declan's voice.

"Well, well, well, if it isn't Cyn Hargrave. I've been looking for you."

~   ~   ~

As soon as the blood started flowing to her legs again, Cyn kept moving. Features composed, she ignored Declan and went straight for the door.

"Hey, I'm talking to you," he said.

She brushed him off like it was nothing more than an unwanted advance. "Sorry, buddy. Not interested."

He followed her onto the street, and she glanced around, desperately looking for an escape. She knew he wasn't going to stop following her.

An alleyway a couple of feet away offered her an option, and Cyn ducked into it. A jagged-edged broken brick on the ground caught her eye, and she grabbed it, hiding it in the folds of her jacket.

Declan followed closely behind, and she turned to face him. "I found your little calling card. Stealing is a crime, though. You of all people should know that."

"So is murder. I know you had something to do with Hunter's death."

Cyn chose her words carefully. "Why would you think that, Declan? I loved Hunter."

"Then why did you gut him in his *sleep*?" He took a step toward her. "His belly was slit open, and his insides were draped across the bed. There was so much blood that some of the first responders on the scene are still torn up over it. Called it one of the worst crime scenes they've ever seen."

Cyn's throat closed up at the memory of all that blood. She couldn't breathe.

Declan took another step toward her. "If you loved him, why did you just leave him there to die? Why, Cyn? Why did you do it?"

"I . . ." She couldn't speak. Couldn't get words out past the lump in her throat.

"I couldn't even be there. Do you know that?" Declan tugged on the ends of his hair with both hands, running his fingers wildly through it. "I couldn't go to the funeral. I was sent away so I wouldn't compromise the case."

With every word, he took another step closer to Cyn. His words were like a hammer, beating her down with every syllable.

He was right—she *did* kill his brother. She was the monster she said he was.

Suddenly, Declan lunged at her and shoved her up against the side of the brick building beside her. Placing his forearm against her throat, he pinned her into place.

"Tell me why I shouldn't kill you right now," he said roughly. "Tell me why I should spare the person who murdered my little brother. The person he said he loved."

He spat the word "love" like it left a foul taste in his mouth.

Cyn just closed her eyes. *Let it be quick. And even though I don't deserve it, please, God, let it be painless.*

"Hey!" someone shouted. "What are you doing? Let go of her!"

Cyn's eyes flew open, and she saw a burly guy running toward them. "Let her go!" he shouted again.

"This isn't over," Declan hissed into her ear.

He dropped his arm and took several steps back. His voice was filled with rage and his hands shook. "I'm going to find you again. And when I do? I'm going to kill you."

Chapter Twenty-Seven

The guy gave chase to Declan but couldn't keep up, so he finally returned to Cyn. "Are you okay? I'm gonna call the cops."

"No! Don't! I mean, that's okay. I'm okay." Cyn thought fast. "That was just an ex-boyfriend. He found out I was dating his . . . roommate. And he wasn't happy about it."

She gave him a wry grin.

"Yeah, well, ex-boyfriend or not, that dude is messed up. He shouldn't be treating you like that. You should still call the cops. Get a restraining order. This one time, my sister—"

Cyn put up a hand and shook her head. "I won't be seeing him again. It'll be fine."

He looked doubtful, so she tried another tactic. "Hey, haven't I seen you before, at the Black Cadillac?" She had no idea if he went to the bar or not but figured by the looks of him that it was a safe-enough bet. "You know Cash, right?"

"Yeah, I know Cash. We ride together sometimes."

"Could you take me there?"

"I'm not sure if the bar is open—"

Cyn turned on the charm and smiled up at him. "It's open."

But the lights were out, and the door was locked when they got to the bar. Cyn's would-be savior gave her a doubtful look. "I don't think—"

"Cash!" Cyn banged on the door. "Open up!"

A light flipped on inside. A second later, the bolt slid free from the other side of the door, and then Cash appeared. "Hey, man." He greeted the biker and they bumped fists.

"Do you know her?" The biker asked, turning to Cyn. "Says she knows you."

From the other night, Cyn willed him to remember. *I was with Thirteen.*

Cash gave her a hard look but then nodded. "Yeah. I know her."

"Some guy was messing with her in the alley. I ran him off,

but she said she didn't want to go to the cops. Wanted to come see you instead."

"Yeah, yeah. I got this. Thanks for bringing her here." Cash stood to the side and gestured for Cyn to come in.

"Thanks for stopping," Cyn said to the biker, who turned to leave. "You're a real sweetheart."

"Anytime, darlin'. Now, you rethink that whole calling-the-cops thing, okay?"

Cyn faked a smile and nodded. Cash nodded too and then shut the door. "Want to tell me what *that* was all about?"

"I'm fine. He just got his facts mixed up."

Cash held up both hands. "Your business, not mine."

Cyn glanced over at the bar. "I know it's early, but how about a drink? I could use one."

"Anything you want. It's on the house."

She turned back to say thanks, but he already had his cell phone to his ear. "Thirteen? It's Cash. Look, I got your girl here at the bar. You need to get down here." He paused and then said, "The, uh . . . you know, the *one*."

"Cyn," she yelled. "My name is Cyn. And I can't *believe* you fucking called him."

She went to the counter and picked out a full bottle of Jack.

If he was going to rat her out, then he sure as shit was going to pay for it with some free booze.

"Yeah, no problem," Cash said, still on the phone. "We'll be here."

He hung up and wisely stayed on the other side of the room until Thirteen showed. Cyn was halfway through the bottle when he got there. He had a scowl on his face, and the door slammed shut behind him.

"I didn't have anything to do with him calling you," Cyn said, gesturing to Cash. "So you can stop giving me that I-just-fucked-up-your-day look. I have Father Montgomery's car. I'll be fine."

"You're not driving."

"Then I'll walk."

"You're not walking, either. Which means we can stay here until you've sobered up, or you can get on my bike and let me take you home. But if we stay? You won't be doing any more drinking." He turned to Cash. "Did you have to give her whiskey?"

Cash shook his head. "Sure. Blame the bartender."

"Damn right I will." Avian turned back to Cyn. "I've made an executive decision. You're coming with me. I can't trust you around him."

Cyn scowled. "Fine. Whatever."

Across the room she could see Cash's smirk as he watched their exchange. She pointed at him. "I'm not going to forget about this, you rat bastard. You owe me a couple more rounds for calling *him*, and you better believe I'll be back to collect."

CHAPTER TWENTY-EIGHT

By the time they made it back to the rectory, cars were starting to fill the church parking lot.

"Shit," Thirteen said. "I forgot about Father Montgomery's funeral."

They went inside the house, and she kept an eye on the church from an upstairs window. She wanted to pay her respects to the priest, but she didn't know what faces she might see at the service. Hampton Falls was a small town.

As the service stretched into the early evening hours, Cyn finally slipped out of the house and went over to the church. One of the double doors was open, and she entered as quietly as she could.

The sanctuary was overflowing with flowers. Dozens and dozens of them. The scent should have been overpowering—roses, carnations, mums, and lilies all competing against each other—but it wasn't.

A priest at the head of the church was leading the congregation through a prayer service, Vespers, if her limited memory of Sunday school when she was younger served her correctly, and Cyn bowed her head, following along as best she could.

When the prayer ended and the congregation stood, Cyn knew it was time for her to leave. As much as she wanted to tell Father Montgomery one last time how much his kindness truly meant to her, she couldn't stay.

It was time to run again.

Hastily making her exit, Cyn went back to the rectory to grab her plants and her suitcase. She was going to take Father Montgomery's car and worry about getting more money along the way. If she had to use her mind mojo to do it, then so be it.

But she didn't make it out before the church emptied and several nuns descended upon the house. They headed straight for the kitchen. She could hear them talking and clinking dishes, and then the smell of food started spreading.

Cyn gave it a couple of minutes and then headed back

upstairs to the attic. She would wait them out there. Leave once everyone was gone. It was only a minor holdup.

And if she got lucky, there might even be leftovers in the fridge to take on the road with her as a snack.

The sound of music woke her. She must have fallen asleep while waiting in the attic, because the sun had gone down. It was pitch black. Cyn listened for any sign of movement downstairs as she waited for her eyes to adjust to the darkness. But the house was still and silent.

Except for that faint drift of music.

It was a string instrument—*violin?*—and she recognized Beethoven's *Moonlight* Sonata. A low note was drawn out, and then it turned into a rapid rise and fall as the strings danced with an audible shiver. It was haunting. The most beautiful thing she'd ever heard.

Cyn followed the sounds outside.

The opening strains of "O Come, O Come, Emmanuel" filled the air, rich and deep with their aching simplicity, and chills washed over her. The musician was a master. She could feel his instrument weeping with sadness. It was there in the hum and quiver of every note.

Closing her eyes, Cyn listened as the music poured through her, invisible notes snaring her in a silken web. The piece was almost unbearable to listen to with all of that passion behind it. When it ended, she was undone. That feeling of being so connected to something outside her body, to something bigger than herself, was something she'd never known she wanted.

And that scared her more than anything.

The last few notes still clung to the air when Cyn glanced up. Thirteen was perched on the edge of the church roof with a cello tucked between his knees. The curve of mahogany vivid in the moonlight, strings the color of faded bone.

Tucking the instrument safely beneath one arm, he jumped to the ground easily. He didn't seem to see her, until she said, "I didn't know you played."

"I don't."

He carried the cello over to a large black case sitting on the ground. It was the one she'd seen in the attic. He put the bow inside, but his fingers lingered on the neck scroll for just a second before he put the cello away too and snapped the locks on the case shut. "That's the last time I'll ever play. I should just get rid of the damn thing."

But he left it there and came to join her.

"Why did you play a Christmas song?" Cyn asked softly.

He took a long time to answer.

"It was Father Montgomery's favorite song. When I found him at the church, he said it was what the angels were singing. I wanted to play it for him one last time."

"You sound like you really loved him."

"I guess I did."

Cyn glanced away and stared down at her feet. "I lost someone I loved too. A couple of months ago, right before I came here. I met this guy after I graduated high school and we moved in together. It was great. *He* was great." She smiled. "His name was Hunter."

Avian paid close attention. Did this have anything to do with the blood and the police sirens he'd seen in her head?

"We met because I tried to steal his car. Well, not *tried* to. I didn't actually steal it. See, when I really want to take someone's car, I just make them give it to me. It's this mind-mojo thing I have. But Hunter had this great Mustang. Rebuilt hemi engine, dual exhaust, and the most amazing red-leather interior you've ever seen. Reminded me a lot of this other car that I boosted in Boston."

Shelley had had a thing for fast cars too. Liked to take them for joy rides. Got in trouble for it a couple of times. But she always managed to sweet talk her way out of anything serious, and then she would be right back at it as soon as another one caught her eye.

Cyn kept talking. "So I was going to take his car, but as soon as I looked at him I just lost it. You know? One look and I was head over heels. Completely gone for this guy. We got together right after that. And then . . . he died. So that's my very long way of saying I know how you feel."

Sticking her hands in her pockets, she turned away from him but then turned back again. Almost hesitantly. "Hey . . . I have something for you. I'm going to go get it, okay?"

She went into the house and returned a couple of minutes later. "Father Montgomery gave me this. But I think you should have it."

Avian stared down at the string of rosary beads lying in the palm of her hand. The sight was like an open wound and a healing balm all at the same time. Father Montgomery had carried them with him every day.

His demon side reacted strongly to the religious artifact— he could feel the burns beneath his skin surfacing, but he kept it in check. Reaching for the beads, he wrapped them around his fist. Ignoring the pain when they touched his skin.

"Thank you," he said, glancing at her. "I don't have anything else to remember him by."

CHAPTER TWENTY-NINE

Cyn knew she was in trouble as soon as he looked at her. His brown eyes desperately searching hers. *Oh, no. No. This isn't good.*

He wrapped the beads around his fist like he was a drowning man and they were the only thing that could possibly save him. When he ducked his head and she heard him whisper, "I miss you, Father," she was lost.

There was something so seductive about suddenly seeing this big, broody guy showing a vulnerable side that Cyn sucked in a sharp breath. God, it was like watching him nuzzle a puppy. It made her want to hold on and never let go.

"Yeah, so . . . I have to go. . . ." She stuttered and took a step back. "Um, to the diner on Twenty-fifth. I have to pick up my paycheck."

Why was she lying to him? She wasn't going to the diner, she was running away again.

"You can use the car," he offered.

"Great, thanks."

"What about that guy who was harassing you?" he said. "I can follow you if you want me to, make sure that he's—"

Hastily, Cyn shook her head. He couldn't follow her. Then he'd know that she was leaving. "I'll be fine. Keys on the kitchen table?"

He nodded, and she had to remind herself not to look back as she walked away from him. Keeping her stride even, she went inside and quickly grabbed the keys.

Her hands were jittery when she started up the car, and she drummed her fingers on the steering wheel, trying to calm down. *Everything's fine. Just go pick up your last paycheck from Marv like you said. Might as well get a couple more bucks before you leave town.*

Cyn made her way to the diner, trying not to think about him holding on to those rosary beads.

The parking lot was full, which meant that inside was going to be a madhouse. Hopefully, she could just slip in, find Marv, get her check, and get out.

Margaret was on duty and so was Dougie Ray. He looked tired. Not used to the shift change from days to nights to cover for her. As soon as he saw her, he perked right up. "Oh, good, now I don't have to work a double—"

Cyn cut him off. "Sorry, Dougie Ray. I'm just here to pick up my check. Family emergency."

He muttered something under his breath about inconsiderate people, but Cyn ignored him and headed straight for the kitchen. That's where she found Marv.

He was working the fryer and yelling at Lenny, but he stopped long enough to give her an angry look. "Mmmmhmm."

"Hey, Marv," she said. "Busy night. That means good things for the register, right?"

"It would mean even better things if I was fully staffed," he barked. "But since you're not in uniform, I'm guessing that ain't gonna happen."

She made her lower lip go all pouty and started blinking rapidly, trying to look like she was holding back tears. "I just got word that my mom is sick. I hate to leave you short handed, but I have to go back home to Ohio. Tonight."

Marv picked up the fry basket from the bubbling grease pit it was submerged in and dumped a dozen golden-brown onion rings onto a waiting plate. "For real?"

"Yeah, for real. Why would I make something like that up?"

He stared at her for a long moment, then said, "Okay."

Cyn felt oddly insulted that he would doubt her. Even though she *was* lying. "I have to take the bus, so that put a serious dent in my savings. I hate to even ask this, but is there any way I could get an advance? I know it's early, but it would really help."

He looked like he was going to say no, so she started blinking faster. "Please, Marv? You'd be doing me a *huge* favor." She had no problem shedding a couple of real tears if she had to.

Marv nodded, a queasy look coming over his face.

Classic. Doesn't know what to do when a girl's going to cry.

Cyn's fake tears turned to a smile. "Thanks. I'll wait right here."

Wiping his hands on his apron, Marv dinged the bell sitting on the pass-through counter and sat the plate of onion rings on it. "Need ya back here, Lenny," he called out.

A minute later, Lenny came and took Marv's place at the fryer, shifting back and forth between it and the griddle as Marv went to get the payroll binder.

"Your mom's sick, huh?" Lenny said, dumping a bag of french fries into the grease.

Cyn crossed the room and opened the industrial-size refrigerator. Last time she checked, there were a couple of Yoo-Hoo bottles in the back. "You heard what I said to Marv?"

"Kind of hard not to. Not exactly private back here, ya know?"

"Tell me about it."

"So, how long are you going to—"

But Lenny didn't finish his question.

"Going to what?" Her back was to him, and she dug deeper in the fridge, moving a carton of eggs to clear a path to the Yoo-Hoo. "Going to be missing you? You know I'll miss you the whole time I'm gone, Lenny." Her fingers finally touched cold glass, and she pulled one of the bottles out. "No, seriously. Going to what?"

When Cyn turned back around again, she saw the reason Lenny didn't answer. Because Declan was there, holding a gun to the side of his head.

CHAPTER THIRTY

As soon as Cyn left, Avian went into the house and poured himself a glass of bourbon. He carried it to the living room and sat in front of the fireplace.

Father Montgomery's rosary was warm against his skin. Already a faint outline etched into his wrist from where the cross pressed against his flesh. But he wasn't going to take it off. It was the only way to keep some part of Father Montgomery alive.

A nagging feeling tugged at Avian, and he took a sip. Hoping to chase the feeling away with the sting of alcohol. But something wasn't right, and he couldn't figure out what it was.

Is it Cyn? Is she okay?

She said she just had to go pick up her paycheck at the diner on Twenty-fifth. He knew where that one was—it was the one he'd followed the cop into.

The same cop who had a rental car and was staying in a motel. Who had a memory of Cyn taking up space inside his head.

He gripped the glass so tightly it shattered in his hand.

Avian shot to his feet and ignored the blood dripping from his fingers. Reaching for the cell phone inside his pocket, he dialed Mint's number as he slammed the front door shut behind him and strode across the yard to the shed.

"Yeeeeellow?" Mint's normal greeting grated on his nerves, and Avian resisted the urge to curse at him.

"Mint, it's me."

"Thirteen! We haven't talked since—"

"Yeah, I know." Avian cut him off. "Listen, I need you to look up a license plate for me."

Mint's tone immediately turned professional. "What do you have?"

"Rental. Out of state."

Avian rattled off the plate from memory, and sixty seconds later Mint had a hit from the database he'd hacked into.

"The car's registered to a Declan Thomas. He has a New

York address. Paid cash, so no credit card to track. But we're not done with Mr. Thomas yet."

Mint was punching something else into the computer. Avian could hear him clicking.

"Wait a minute. Wait just a minute." Mint suddenly let out a low whistle, and Avian switched the phone to his other hand as he started up his bike.

"What?"

"It's not good."

"Just tell me, Mint. I don't have time to fuck around."

"Well, to start with, Declan Thomas used to be a cop."

"Used to be?" Avian pulled out of the shed and headed toward the diner.

"Yeah. He was with the NYPD in Manhattan for two years. But he lost his badge a couple months ago. Right around the time his little brother was murdered."

A sick feeling hit Avian in his gut. He knew what Mint was going to say next.

"The brother's name was Hunter. Thomas was apparently under investigation for a couple of brutality incidents before all that, but his brother's death seemed to be the thing that set him off. He was committed to a voluntary ninety-day program at a psychiatric hospital for evaluation. But he checked himself out after a week."

Hunter was the name of the dead boyfriend Cyn mentioned, and Declan was his brother. A crazy ex-cop obsessed with finding his kid brother's killer, and a sudden interest in Cyn.

He'd bet his right arm that that wasn't a coincidence.

"You know this guy?" Mint asked.

"Yeah. And that's not even the complicated part." Avian hit the highway and accelerated. He was still ten minutes away from the diner. *Too far.*

"I know you don't need me to tell you this, but be careful, man."

"Noted."

Avian's voice was hard.

Mint got the message loud and clear. "Anything more you need from me?"

"That's it."

"Good luck with him, then. And call me sometime when you don't have a crazy cop on your hands, okay? Better yet, come down and see me before—"

But Avian didn't hear what Mint said. He'd already hung up the phone.

CHAPTER THIRTY-ONE

The Yoo-Hoo bottle Cyn was holding hit the floor, and glass flew everywhere. She flinched at the sound. Lenny's eyes were wide with fear.

"If this is about Hunter," she said, "then let's talk. Just you and me. Leave Lenny out of it."

"Oh, yeah, we're going to talk about Hunter." Declan pressed the barrel of the gun tightly against Lenny's temple. "But not here."

"Do you think you'll be back for the—" Marv was looking down at the payroll binder as he came out of his office but stopped short when he saw what was going on. "Holy shit, man. What are you *doing?* I thought you were a cop? Put the gun down."

While Declan was distracted by Marv, Cyn realized that she was standing beside the box of mangled spoons the disposal had chewed up and spit back out again. Several of them were so twisted, they resembled ice picks more than silverware. She nudged the edge of the chair beside her so that it tipped over. Declan shot her a glare. "Sorry," she said quickly. "I get clumsy when I'm nervous."

Bending over to pick up the chair, Cyn grabbed one of the spoon remnants and shoved it in her pocket. It wasn't much, but at least it was something.

Declan glanced back over at Marv. "I needed to have a little chat with one of your waitresses here and had to do something to get her attention. She didn't make my burger right."

"There's no need for any of this," Marv replied. "We can get you a new burger right now, on the house. What do you want on it? Lettuce? Onions? Tomat—"

"It's not about a burger, Marv," Cyn said.

The stench of burning french fries permeated the air, adding to the tension in the room.

"She's right about that." Declan pulled the gun back slightly. "I appreciate the offer, though. I'll have to take you up on it next time. Now I think me and Cyn here need to find someplace a little more private to talk."

"She's not going anywhere with you," Marv rebutted.

But Cyn was already nodding her agreement. *Whatever it takes to get you to put the gun down.* "Yeah, sure."

Marv turned to face her. "Cynsation, you don't have to do this."

"We're just going to talk. Right?" she asked Declan.

"Of course," Declan promised, but the smile on his face told a different story.

All I have to do is get the gun as far away from Marv and Lenny as possible. I don't care what he does to me. I just can't let anyone else get hurt. "Okay. Let's go."

Declan gestured for Cyn to come to him and grabbed a fistful of Lenny's shirt to move him out of her way. Lenny had just put up both hands, to show that he was going to comply, when Margaret burst through the swinging door, yelling that she needed her fries for table twelve, and caught sight of Declan.

"Oh my God!" she screamed. "He's got a gun!"

She immediately fell to her knees and covered her head with her hands, begging to be able to see her children again.

"Am I pointing this gun at you, sweetheart?" Declan said. "*No.* So calm the fuck down." He aimed it in Cyn's direction again. "*You* get over here. Nobody else move."

When Cyn didn't move fast enough, Declan cocked the hammer. "Let's get this shit rolling. I don't have all day."

Everything happened in a split second after that. Cyn started toward Declan, and he gave Lenny a hard shove in the direction of the fryer. Lenny lost his balance and skidded on the linoleum floor, landing face first in the boiling grease.

Screams of pain filled the air, mingling with the scent of burning flesh and scorched potatoes, and Marv went running to Lenny, trying to haul him out by the waistband of his pants. Lenny kept screaming and thrashing, so Marv couldn't get a firm grip. Finally, he yanked on Lenny's shirt so hard, it ripped.

They both collapsed in a heap on the floor.

"You're gonna be fine," Marv kept saying, trying to comfort him. "It's not that bad. You're gonna be fine."

Margaret was wailing in the corner, and Declan shook his head in disgust at the scene in front of him. He pushed Cyn toward the back door with the muzzle of his gun. "Outside."

Her feet started to move on their own, and she willed Marv to look up. To let her know that Lenny really was going to be fine. That everything really was going to be okay.

But Marv was too busy trying to hold the peeling skin of his employee's face together.

Declan followed Cyn to the door and shoved the gun into her ribs. Propelling her toward a side street, he walked closely beside her to hide his lethal motivation from any witnesses.

They came to a white car, and he made her get in the driver's seat while he kept the gun trained on her.

He instructed her to start the car and drive. Cyn just concentrated on keeping her eyes on the road. They passed a junkyard, and he told her to stop. "Go back. Pull in there."

Cyn pulled up to the padlocked gates marked PETE'S SALVAGE YARD. It was after hours, and they were clearly closed.

"Get out," Declan said.

Cyn followed his instructions, discreetly looking around to see if there was any way to escape. She almost jumped out of her skin when he suddenly shot the lock off the gate. "Jesus Christ! Give me some warning next time. You scared the shit out of me."

Declan laughed and roughly grabbed her arm. Dragging her behind him, he nudged one of the heavy gates open just far enough so they could squeeze through.

Walking into the junkyard immediately made Cyn claustrophobic. It was a graveyard for cars. Half-buried in the ground like forgotten tombstones, rusty vehicles loomed in shadows all around her. Busted glass and bits of metal crunched beneath her feet.

"It's quiet," Declan said, glancing around. "I like that." He wandered over to the raised trunk of an old car and pushed it down. The sound of heavy metal clunking shut echoed ominously around them. "Unless the smell got to be too bad, no one would find a body left here for a long, long time."

Cyn tried to tamp down the sense of panic springing up inside her. *He's going to kill me and leave me here.*

"You should have just followed through with your plan at the gas station. That would have made everything easier." Declan walked back around to the front of the car and opened the driver's side door.

"What plan at the gas station?"

He reached under the dashboard. A second later, the latch on the trunk made a popping noise. "To shoot yourself."

"I don't know what you mean."

He stood back up and said, "Trunk. Now."

Cyn hesitated. She wasn't going to sign her own death warrant *that* easily. But Declan shoved the gun up against her forehead.

"Do you really want this to get messy?" he said in a calm voice. "Don't make me ask again."

Cyn slowly moved toward the car. "What . . ." Her voice cracked, and she had to try again. "What did you mean, my plan to shoot myself?"

"I saw you at the gas station." Declan gestured to the trunk. "*Go* on." He waited until she climbed in before he spoke again.

"You had a gun to your head but didn't pull the trigger. Couldn't go through with it, huh?"

Cyn shifted to her side and pulled her knees up. *I put the gun to my head? Why didn't Thirteen tell me that?*

Something sharp poked her shoulder, and she put one hand behind her to move whatever it was. Cold metal registered against her fingertips, and she realized it was a tire iron. A blunt, heavy tire iron.

She had to move fast. She'd dug her own grave now—but she had no intention of lying in it.

"You're right," Cyn said, her fingers wrapping around the tire iron. She tensed up. "I guess I couldn't go through with it." She purposefully lowered her voice. "So you can fuck off."

"What's that?" Declan bent down so he could hear what she said.

"I said, *fuck off*, asshole." Cyn sat up and swung the tire iron. It was so heavy, her shoulder muscles screamed at the motion, but she held on and took aim at Declan's mouth. The tire iron connected, and a spray of blood and teeth erupted from his face.

Declan stumbled backward and landed flat on his back. The gun flew from his hand. He made a wet, gurgling noise as he lay on the ground, and Cyn listened to him for just a second before her brain suddenly kicked into gear. *Go! Go! Go!*

Cyn climbed out of the trunk as fast as she could. She wasted precious time scanning the ground for the gun, but the landscape was too overrun with littered car parts for her to find it.

Forget it, just go!

Cyn turned back around to head for the gates, but something suddenly blocked her path.

She saw red eyes first, and then the rest of him. Lips pulled back to reveal wicked-looking teeth, massive paws, and broad shoulders. It was a guard dog. The biggest, meanest, nastiest-looking guard dog she'd ever seen. And it was staring right at her.

Declan made a noise somewhere between a yell and a groan, and she knew it wouldn't be long until he got up again. She was running out of time.

Cyn stared down the dog. *Just let me go. Eat him. He'll make a tasty snack.*

As if on cue, the dog's spine stiffened, and the hair on its back rose up.

She almost thought she saw smoke coming off of it.

With a growl that rumbled deep from its belly, the dog sprang into action and covered the distance between her and Declan with a single leap. Declan's groans turned to screams, and Cyn couldn't stop herself from shuddering at the sound of bones crunching and flesh ripping. Taking advantage of the opportunity, she ran as fast as she could for the gate.

She never even realized that Declan had found his gun again and she should have been looking behind her.

CHAPTER THIRTY-TWO

Cyn made it to the gates and squeezed her way through before stopping to catch her breath. *I have to get to Thirteen. He'll know what to do about Declan.*

The car was less than ten feet away. Cyn stood up and slowly walked over to it. *Keys! Where did I put the goddamn keys?* Then she realized that they were still in the ignition. Declan didn't take them when he made her get out.

A hysterical laugh threatened to spill out of her, but Cyn clamped her mouth shut and mutely shook her head as she slid behind the wheel. "This is what happens when you don't follow through with your plan, Declan," she said out loud. "It makes everything easier."

She put the car in reverse and was just about to back up when an odd clanking sound came from the rear passenger-side door.

"Shit."

Cyn slammed on her brakes and mulled over what she should do.

The sound came again.

"What the fuck *is* that?" Cyn already had her door halfway open, determined to see what she'd hit, when the back door suddenly opened.

Declan's eyes met hers in the rearview, and she saw him propping a bloody left arm up against the backseat as he dragged himself the rest of the way into the car. With his right hand, he lifted the gun to the back of her head.

"Drive," he mumbled.

His top lip was split into two pieces—part of it hanging down the side of his cheek like a hunk of dead meat—and his upper and lower front teeth were gone. A nasty black and blue bruise circled his nose. The veins in his face were discolored, pulsing like throbbing black caterpillars. He turned his head and spit out a mouthful of red-tinted foam.

There was no time for panic. Cyn's brain had gone past that now and was operating only on sheer logic. "Where?"

"The falls. Just go straight, it's not far."

Cyn put the car in gear and pulled away from the salvage yard. She knew now there was no escaping him. Declan was going to kill her. It was just a matter of how long it would take, and how painful it would be.

When the wooded area that led to the falls came into view, Cyn turned onto the road that would take them to their final destination. The road gave way to a path, and at the end of the path was the bluff. The sound of rushing water was loud enough to drown out the car's engine.

Declan used the gun again to prompt Cyn to get out and prodded her closer to the water's edge. He stumbled behind her and almost fell but managed to catch himself at the last second.

Cyn glanced around. "How did you know about this place?"

"Followed you from the gas station."

He saw me with Thirteen. "Then you should probably know that I don't put out on the first date. Just FYI." She crossed her arms but realized what else it meant that he'd followed them that night. "Did you overhear our conversation?"

"Part of it."

"Which part?"

"The part that means I know all about you being an Echo. Is that why you killed Hunter? Because you don't have a soul?"

"Don't have a soul? I—"

"You're some kind of soul freak. I heard that guy telling you."

"I don't know what you think you heard, but you sound crazy."

At the mention of the word "crazy," Declan grew agitated and started waving the gun around. "Crazy? *I'm* not fucking crazy. Do you understand that? I'm not stupid, either. Of course, you wouldn't confess something like that to me. It sounds crazy because it is. But I know all about crazy. And I know other ways to get you to confess your sins to me."

He dropped the arm holding the gun to his side. Cyn tried not to flinch as he suddenly moved closer. Little flecks of blood flew out of his mouth as he sneered, "I also know how to make you beg."

"You want to hear someone beg?" a voice said from behind them. "I'll get right on that."

Cyn turned around to see Thirteen standing there, the large black dog from the junkyard next to him.

Ears back, hair raised, every single one of the dog's razorlike teeth showed as its lips curled in a snarl. Steam rose from its fur in wisps that matched the smoke rising off of Thirteen. Vivid burn marks covered Thirteen's arms, and his red eyes and horns were in full effect. He was six feet five inches of badass mixed with pissed-off motherfucker.

"What *are* you?" Declan said.

Thirteen just glared at him. "Really? Are you going to make me say it?"

"Yeah, I'm going to make you say it. *What* the *fuck* are you?"

"Your worst nightmare."

He took a step forward, and Declan turned the gun on Cyn. "Don't get any ideas. This is between me and her."

Thirteen took another step closer. "What did she do to you?"

"She killed my little brother! He was stabbed in his own bed. And *she* was *there*."

"Doesn't mean she did it."

Declan tilted his head toward him, like he was sharing a secret. "I heard what you told her the other night. She's an Echo. That's why she did it. Some sort of satanic ritual or something."

"Okay." Thirteen nodded like he was in full agreement. "But do you have any proof that she killed him? You were a cop. You know you need proof."

Cyn glanced over at Thirteen. "*Was?* He *was* a cop? He told me he's with the Sleepy Hollow Police Department."

"So I fucking lied," Declan said. Distracted, he lowered the gun. "I was with the NYPD and they put me on suspension."

"Maybe you just pissed off the wrong person." Thirteen looked Declan straight in the eye. "You're with the Navarro coven, right? Vampires know a lot of interesting ways to get a message across. They can be pretty brutal."

Cyn tried to follow what Thirteen was saying. *Vampires are real too? And Declan is working with them?*

"We have an understanding," Declan argued. "I make sure no one ever notices when they do their thing, and in exchange, they'll turn me. I've always held up my end—they have no reason to come after me or my brother."

"They're sharing their blood with you?"

Declan nodded, then started coughing uncontrollably. Doubled over, he fought to bring the gun back up so it was pointed at Cyn, but his hand was shaking. The black veins in his face bulged with every wheeze and seemed to be growing larger. When Cyn glanced down at his hand, she saw the veins there were turning black too. Traveling up his arms like they were carrying black ink.

"What's wrong with me?" Declan finally said.

Thirteen gestured at the gaping wound covering Declan's shoulder. "Looks like a dog bite to me."

"I fought him off." Declan glared over at the large dog, who was keeping silent watch. "Hit him with the butt of my gun. Should have been enough to crack his skull."

"It probably was," Thirteen said. "He heals fast. Like me."

"So, am I infected?" Declan glanced back down at his black veins. "Is he some kind of . . . werewolf or something?"

"Hellhound. Let's just say you don't have to worry about turning into a vampire anymore. Hell, you don't have to worry about *anything* anymore. Time's up."

Thirteen took one more step and was finally close enough to reach out and take the gun.

Cyn could tell that he was going to go for it, but instead of waiting for him to make his move she reached for the sharpened spoon in her pocket. She wasn't done with Declan yet.

Quickly counting to three, she pulled it out and jabbed it over her shoulder. Right where Declan was standing. Slight resistance gave way to a gelatinous substance, and then a sudden spurt of warm blood against the back of her head and Declan's howl of pain let her know that her aim was true: She'd hit him in the eye.

Declan's gun dropped to the ground with a dull thud. "You fucking bitch!" he spit out.

Blood was pouring down his face, and something flashed dark and deadly in his good eye.

In that instant, Cyn knew what he was going to do.

Declan reached out and sunk both hands into her shoulders, hauled her up against him, and then stepped off the edge of the bluff.

Chapter Thirty-Three

Cyn screamed as they went over, and Avian's wings burst out of his jacket. With two strong pumps, he was over the side of the cliff and diving down after her.

The spray of water from the falls was almost strong enough to knock him off course, but he reached out to snag her ankle and managed to stop them midfall. Their combined weight made it cumbersome to navigate, and he fought to pull them back up over the cliff.

"Get *off* of *me*," he heard Cyn grunting, and he looked down to see her kicking at Declan.

The cop's face was a mangled mess—one eye bloody and bulging, his lip split into two, broken capillaries and blood vessels covering his face and arms. The hellhound's bite had done a considerable amount of damage.

But so had Cyn.

She kicked one more time, and Declan started coughing again. His body convulsed as he struggled for air. With one final heave, she knocked him loose.

Avian leveled off, and they both watched Declan's body free-fall into the water below. He disappeared and then resurfaced, bobbing lifelessly until the current carried him over the falls. If there was any question as to whether or not he could have survived, it was answered as his body was dashed against the rocks at the bottom of the waterfall over and over again.

Avian cleared the edge of the bluff and let go of Cyn's ankle as soon as the ground was close enough for them to land safely. He came to a stop several feet away. The scars on his back were burning like a son of a bitch, and he fought to keep himself under control.

"Holy shit, Thirteen," Cyn said. "I was just getting used to the horns. You can *fly*?!"

She came closer, and he arched backward, hissing with pain. "*Don't.* Don't come near me."

The burns on Avian's arms deepened, like someone was branding him with a hot poker from the inside, and his horns throbbed with a painful intensity. When he got pissed off, the demon side of him wanted to do some damage. Regardless of what, or *who*, was around.

That's how he'd gotten the scar from Shelley. When he wasn't careful, and the demon side had slipped out. Luckily, she'd been smart enough to use the knife she'd always carried and had nicked the side of his neck just below his left ear. He'd been distracted enough by it to rein himself back in.

"What's happening to you?" Cyn asked. "It looks . . . painful."

Avian contorted as the burns flared up again, and he landed hard with one knee on the ground. He didn't answer her question. It took all of his willpower to make sure his demon side stayed under wraps.

Eventually his horns receded to nubs, and he changed his eye color back to brown. The wings were another matter— they would have to wait until he could bind them again.

When he stood, Cyn glanced at his arms and the fading scars left behind. "Happens when I get angry," he offered by way of explanation. "I burn from the inside out. It's my curse."

"So the burn marks are coming from the *inside* and pushing their way *out* of your skin?"

He nodded.

She looked at his shoulders. "And *that's*"—she gestured to the black feathers sprouting from his shoulder blades—"all part of this too?"

"They come from my mother's side of the family."

"Wings *and* horns." She turned away from him, then turned back with a confused expression on her face. "Have they always been there?"

"Always."

"I didn't feel them when I rode behind you on your bike."

"I keep them bound."

Cyn gave him a brief, sweeping glance. "Anything else I should know about? Any other surprises?"

Besides the healing, shape shifting, persuasion, memory reading, and general-ass-kicking skills?

Avian shook his head. "Nope. That's it." Removing his jacket, he folded his wings down and then put the jacket back on.

"Okay. Good. But you and I are going to have a little chat when we get back to the house." She glanced around and absentmindedly rubbed her arms. Her clothing was wet from coming so close to the waterfall.

"My bike is back where the road ends," he said, answering her unasked question. "I didn't want to lose the element of surprise, so I left it there."

He put two fingers to his mouth and whistled. The hellhound followed them back to the bike.

"What's with the dog?" Cyn asked, climbing behind him. She was careful not to touch his wings. "He was at the junkyard Declan made me go to."

"He's a hellhound. A guardian of the dead. I passed by the junkyard when I was out looking for you and saw the dog heading in this direction. Since the cop was drinking blood from the undead, the hellhound was able to follow his scent."

Cyn shrugged. "Whatever he is, I'm glad he was there. He slowed down Declan enough for me to get a head start."

The hellhound raced beside them the whole way back to Pete's Salvage Yard. Keeping up an easy pace. When they reached the gates, he leapt over them and disappeared inside.

They rode in silence the rest of the way back to the rectory, and Avian let Cyn off at the kitchen door before putting his bike away. He didn't realize that she hadn't gone inside yet but was still watching him when he dropped the torn jacket into a heap on the ground and set his wings free.

"Hey!" Cyn suddenly called. "Are you going up there?" She pointed to the roof of the church.

"Yeah," Avian said, and cursed himself for even *thinking* what he was going to say next. "Wanna come?"

Chapter Thirty-Four

Cyn didn't give herself any time to think before she nodded. She took a step toward him. "So, we just . . . go up?"

"We just go up."

Pushing aside her fear of heights, Cyn closed the gap between them. She could feel the warmth radiating off of him. It was like having her own personal heater.

Thirteen snaked an arm around her waist and pulled her tightly against his chest. "So you don't fall," he said.

Heat rushed to her head. *It doesn't mean anything.*

But that didn't stop her from wrapping her arms around him in return.

The ground suddenly let go of her feet, and she looked

down. They were rising higher and higher. *Oh my God, we're flying!*

They crested above the roof of the church, and he glided down to an overhang with a ledge. The narrow ledge offered enough room for one person to stand, but with two it was a tight fit. Cyn shifted her weight to let go of him, but her foot was too close to the edge, and she jerked off balance.

Thirteen's grip around her waist tightened, and he pulled her back. "I got you."

"Can I just . . . ?" Cyn asked before wrapping her arms tighter around him. He was ridiculously warm—*No, not warm. Hot. Oh my God, he is* so *hot*—and she could feel his well-defined chest move slowly up and down beneath her ear as he inhaled and exhaled. Something hung around his neck under his T-shirt, a medallion of some kind, and he could feel it next to her cheek.

"What's this?" she asked, reaching for it without even thinking.

Thirteen's hand slid down and covered her wandering fingers. She pulled away, and he removed the necklace from his shirt. He glanced down at it, and in the moonlight Cyn could see it was a rectangular piece of bronze metal with words carved into it.

"'Every saint has a past, and every sinner has a future,'" he said. "Oscar Wilde. It was a quote Father Montgomery used to say to me, so I had this made."

"Nice thought, but it's not true."

"The saint part? Or the sinner part?"

"The sinner part." Cyn glanced up at the stars. They were so close. "Some sins are too big to ever recover from."

"Are you talking from experience?"

His voice rumbled against the ear she had pressed to his chest. "Yeah. I am."

He stayed quiet, and Cyn contemplated whether or not she should spill her secret. He'd said that he knew what it was like to wish he could take something back. Maybe he'd understand what it was like to carry such a weight on her shoulders all the time too.

Taking a deep breath, Cyn said softly, "Declan was right about his brother. I murdered Hunter."

She waited for him to pull away. To stare down at her with horror. She'd just admitted to committing a major crime.

But he didn't say anything.

Cyn felt compelled to fill the awkward silence. "I don't know what Declan was involved in, but it didn't have anything to do with his brother. I woke up next to Hunter in bed, covered in his blood, and I . . . I panicked. He wouldn't wake up, and there was a knife on the floor, so I took it with me and threw it into a river on my way out of town. I don't know why I didn't stay. I guess I didn't want to go to jail."

He still didn't say anything.

"So you see why I don't believe that every sinner has a future, right?" she said. "At least, I certainly don't. Unless you mean a future filled with constantly running. Always looking over my shoulder and wondering when the cops are going to finally catch up with me."

She looked up at him and gripped the edges of his shirt, almost desperately. "Are you going to say anything? I just admitted to killing my boyfriend, and you haven't even blinked."

"I'm sure you had your reasons."

"What?" Cyn shook her head. "You're sure I had my *reasons* for killing Hunter? And what would those be?"

Thirteen stared down at her. "I don't know. But I live in a world that's not black and white. There's a lot of gray."

"And you think this is just one of those gray areas?"

He didn't tell her that when she reached for his necklace and he touched her fingers, he got another flash of the scene with Hunter. Just like when he'd woken her up from the bad dream when she was sleeping on the couch, there was no actual *memory* of the killing.

Just the after.

"Yeah. I do." His gaze shifted to her mouth, and suddenly another memory was filling his head. The memory of what she tasted like.

"Stop looking at me like that," she said crossly.

"Like what?"

"Like you're going to kiss me again."

Damn. His pride was actually stung a bit by that one. "Was it that bad? Shelley never—"

His tone changed when he said her name, and Cyn glanced up at the trace of longing that was still there. "Who's Shelley?"

"She was someone I loved."

"Did something happen to her?"

"She was an Echo, and she died."

His jaw flexed, and she could tell that he was clenching his teeth.

"Why did you come looking for me?" Cyn said suddenly.

Thirteen held her gaze. "I knew the cop was bad news. I made a call to a friend of mine and found out the cop had a brother named Hunter who was killed. I put two and two together. Figured it was your Hunter."

"That's all there was to it? Nothing . . . more?"

Before he could answer, she said, "Because that kiss didn't mean anything to me. I want you to know that."

He glanced away, and at the same time a crack of thunder came from overhead. A slight breeze blew across the roof of the church, and Cyn shivered. Even being this close to him, she was still cold.

"Let's go inside the house before the rain starts," he finally said. "And it didn't mean anything to me, either. I don't get involved with Echos."

CHAPTER THIRTY-FIVE

Cyn forced herself to let go of Thirteen as soon as her feet touched the ground. It was good that the kiss didn't mean anything to him. That meant they could skip the awkward do-you-or-don't-you-have-feelings-for-me part.

They went inside the house, and he went straight to the coffeemaker. "Wouldn't some whiskey be better?" Cyn suggested.

"Maybe later."

Although she would have preferred a shot of Jack to warm her up, she had to admit, some fresh coffee sounded good. "Irish coffee?"

"I'm not Irish." He ground up some coffee beans, and Cyn sat down at the table.

"Speaking of not being Irish. What exactly *are* you? You said you have a demon side, but why the wings? And why are they black?"

"I'm half demon, half angel."

Cyn felt her eyes go wide. "You . . . *are*? Part angel? Seriously?"

The coffee started percolating, and he joined her at the table. "My father was a demon, my mother was an angel. I don't know why my wings are black instead of white. They just are."

"Is that what a Revenant is—half angel, half demon?"

"No. I'm the only one like me."

"But there *are* other Revenants out there? Just not like you?"

"The other Revenants are reapers. When the earth was first formed, there were originally six teams to help with reaping human souls. Each team was made up of one angel and one demon. To make sure heaven and hell were equally represented."

"Originally?"

The coffeemaker beeped, and he stood up. "Over time, humans started multiplying like rabbits, and the six teams of reapers weren't enough. So they started working exclusively with Shades. Shades are the only humans allowed to stay on earth after they've died. They're keepers of sacred burial grounds, cemeteries, sanctuaries."

He pulled down two mugs from the cabinet and poured steaming black liquid into each one. "Shades have to find their other half during their lifetime in order to do their job as guardians. After they find their partner, Revenants help them cross over after death to become these gatekeepers."

Cyn reached for her cup, shrugging away his offer of milk and sugar, and wrapped her hands around it. "But you said 'originally.' Does that mean there are more than six teams of Revenants now? Are there different Revenants?"

"When the original teams got tired of doing their job, they recruited Shades to take their place. So there are more than six teams of Revenants now, but none of them are the original angels and demons."

"And you were never part of these teams. That's why you're Thirteen. You were the odd one out."

His grip tightened on the handle of his cup. "I was just a mistake made when a demon seduced an angel. Two Revenants fucked up, and I was the end result."

"So that makes you . . ."

"Very old."

"Wow." Cyn took a sip of her coffee. Then she said, "So why don't you do the Revenant job too? Help these Shades cross over?"

"I stay out of their way, and they stay out of mine. To say there's no love lost between me and the other Revenants would be an understatement."

"Why?"

"Because they don't like that I do my own thing. But if they're not going to neuter the vamps, tramps, and demons that are out there, then I will. Someone has to."

"So you hunt monsters? Judge, jury, and executioner style?"

"You could say that."

"*Anything* that's supernatural you just . . . get rid of?"

"Not everything. I make exceptions."

"I guess that's why you wear black all the time, then." She grinned at him. "To match your soul."

"I wear black because it hides bloodstains better."

"Ah, I should have known." Cyn went to set her cup down on the table, but it slipped out of her hands.

Thirteen caught it before it fell.

"Thanks." She glanced down at his outstretched arm. It was the one covered in ink. A small "13" was tattooed near his wrist. The word *treize* was above it, *tredici* below it. Other words and symbols crisscrossed his arm: *Tretten, dreizehn, tizenhárom, treisprezece, treze* . . .

"Do these all mean 'thirteen'?" Cyn asked. She knew some

French and Italian from the eight high schools she'd bounced around between while her mom chased boyfriends.

He nodded. "One for every language that I know." Her eyebrows shot up in surprise as she looked at his completely covered arm again. "I know a lot of languages."

Cyn snorted and took the coffee cup back from him. Standing, she took it over to the sink and rinsed it out. "So, since you know so much about languages and Revenants, do you know anything else about Echos? More specifically, what I have to look forward to? Is it just going to be one soul popping in after another and frequent blackouts for the rest of my life?"

She turned to face him. "Declan said something to me about following me the night I went to the gas station and seeing the gun. He said I had it to my temple. Like I was going to pull the trigger. Did you know about that? Did you see that in my memories when you read me?"

He gave her a hard look. "Don't ask questions you don't want to know the answers to."

"Oh, I want to know. Believe me, I want to know. So, is that a yes? Do I have a death wish or something? Did I try to commit *suicide*?"

"It was the soul inside you. He wants out."

"*He?* Do you know who it is?"

"His name is Grifyth, but he likes to call himself Vincent now."

Something twitched in the back of Cyn's brain, and she tried to place it. "I know that name," she mumbled. "I know that name from somewhere. I know that name. . . ."

"He said a Shade crossover in Sleepy Hollow went wrong, and that's when he found himself inside you."

Sleepy Hollow. Where my fucked-up memories include a bridge and a dead girl named Abbey. "How do you know all of this?"

"He told me."

Cyn almost dropped her cup. "He *told* you?" Her voice rose. "When was this? And why didn't you tell me sooner?"

"It happened when you blacked out in the kitchen. And I'm telling you now."

She glared at him. "So you've known all along who this soul inside of me is and that he wants to escape so badly, he's willing to get rid of me to do it, yet you figured you'd just wait until now to tell me."

He shrugged.

"Why does he want out?"

"Because no Echo has ever been able to withstand more than seven souls passing through them. It's too hard on the mortal body. You've had four souls inside you. He's number five."

"*Seven?* And I'm already on number *five?*" Cyn started to pace. "What can we do? I don't want him to just keep taking over and making me try to hurt myself."

He was quiet for a moment, and Cyn felt her desperation growing. Finally, he said, "There is one thing I could try. But it involves going back to the last place he was corporeal."

Cyn bit her lip. *Go back to Sleepy Hollow? Where the cops might still be looking for me? I could end up in jail. . . . Then again, if I don't at least try, I'll be stuck with him until the next soul comes along. Or until he finally manages to finish the job. . . .*

"What would you have to do?"

Chapter Thirty-Six

Cyn tried to take in what Thirteen was saying, but she couldn't wrap her head around it. "Okay, so wait, tell me again how this would work?"

He leaned forward. "I could force him out. Make him give up his space and move on to the afterlife."

"Have you ever done that before?"

"No."

"So, what if it doesn't work?"

"You end up right back where you are now."

Except I could piss off this Vincent soul inside me. If he's angry and wants out now, *what happens when this doesn't work and we're stuck with each other? What will he try to do then?*

"I need to think about it," Cyn heard herself saying. Her head was starting to hurt, and she just wanted someplace quiet to think. "I'm going to take a shower."

Heading upstairs, she grabbed some clean clothes from her suitcase. But she couldn't find a pair of socks. "I know I have, like, eight pairs in here," Cyn muttered, searching through the suitcase. She dug all the way to the bottom but stopped when her hand hit something hard.

It was the knife she'd hidden in the back of the toilet, wrapped up in an old towel.

I forgot all about this.

As soon as she touched it, a flashback hit her.

Bloody handle. Bloody blade. There's so much blood everywhere. Where did it come from? Crying, moaning, pleading. No, it's a whisper. A prayer. Have to hide the knife. Don't let anyone know you have it—

Cyn jerked back and dropped the blade. *Not again. Please, not again.*

The blood. The prayer. The tears . . .

It was Father Montgomery.

She was the one who'd killed Father Montgomery.

The whole time she was showering, Cyn tried to rationalize herself through the situation. Did she *really* kill him? Was the knife the murder weapon? And if so, why? *Why?*

It just didn't make any sense.

After the shower, Cyn hid the knife back in her suitcase and then quickly got dressed. When she went downstairs, Thirteen was standing in front of her plants by the window. He had a small cup in one hand and was watering the ficus tree. Her stomach somersaulted.

She had to tell him.

Cyn stepped forward, but he shifted to the side and she could see a phone next to his ear.

"Yeah, thanks," she heard him say. "Get back to me if anything comes up."

After he gets Vincent out. I'll tell him after he gets Vincent out of me. I can't afford any distractions right now, and telling him that I was the one who killed his surrogate father is a big fucking distraction.

He snapped the phone shut and glanced back at her. Cyn awkwardly crossed and uncrossed her arms. Trying to affect a casual stance. "Who was that?"

"The police investigating Father Montgomery's murder." He said it with a slight change in his tone, and Cyn got the feeling that he wasn't being completely truthful with her.

"Do they, uh, have any leads?" She had to fight to keep her own voice steady. "Any ideas who did it?"

"Nothing that they're willing to talk about with me." He moved over to the stove, and Cyn realized then that something was cooking. "I think they're under the impression that I'd take matters into my own hands if I knew who did it. They're not wrong."

"Oh." Cyn twisted her ring nervously.

The tantalizing smell of cheddar cheese, apples, and bacon filled the room, and Thirteen flipped something up out of a frying pan and caught it in midair.

"How did he die?" she said suddenly. "I mean, I was there right afterward, and it looked like his face was bruised. Was he beaten? Strangled?"

Thirteen cast her a quick glance. "Stabbed."

Oh, God. Her stomach completely sank to the floor.

She reached up to tug on the back of her wig, and he saw her.

"No need for that. Your wig came off when you were sleeping on the couch. Secret's out: You're a ginger."

"I don't want to advertise that fact, so let's keep it under wraps, okay?"

She glanced at the table, and it took her a second to realize an empty plate was sitting there. He brought the pan over and slid a golden brown grilled cheese onto it. Tender apple wedges peeked out of its crispy edges, melted cheddar oozed from the sides, and the bacon was the exact shade of burnt she liked.

"Eat," he said, holding the plate up to her. She almost wavered.

But then everything came crashing back to her. "What are you *doing*?" Cyn asked.

"Making you food. I thought you might be hungry. Something wrong with that?"

"Yes, there's something wrong with that."

She didn't deserve this. She didn't deserve him doing something nice when she was purposely hiding something terrible from him just so she could use him. "I didn't *ask* you to make me food. I didn't ask you to—"

"Calm down. It's just a damn sandwich."

"I can't have you making me grilled cheese!" Cyn exploded. Turning her back on the sandwich, she went over to the kitchen door. "I want to go back to Sleepy Hollow. *Now.* I want this thing done and over with."

Before they could go, Cyn had to say good-bye to her plants. Avian waited as she whispered something to each one of them.

"Where did you learn that?" he asked when they were finally on their way out of the house.

"Learn what?"

"What you just said. It was a Gaelic blessing of growth and peace."

Cyn shrugged. "I don't know. Ever since I was young, I've had this special bond with plants. The words are just things that I see in my head."

"It probably came from one of your souls. Maybe someone was a botanist. Or a witch."

She climbed on the motorcycle behind him but sat too far back.

"I know you don't want to touch my wings, but you're going to have to sit closer than that," Avian said. "I don't want to have to stop to pick you up if you fall off."

"*Me* not want to touch your wings? I thought *you* didn't want me to touch your wings. I thought it was an etiquette thing. I was just trying to be nice."

"Stop trying to be nice and just move closer, okay?"

She scooted forward a couple of inches and wrapped her arms around him as he made a quick call to a guy named Joe. Joe owed him one. Avian had helped his sister and her boyfriend find a safe place to live. Which wasn't easy to do since they were both Orthos demons who needed dank water and lots of moss.

They made good time on the road to New York, and four hours later Avian pulled into the driveway of the address Joe had given him and turned off his bike. Cyn stayed quiet.

Joe came out of the house a couple of minutes later, wearing a scowl and an oversize coat. "I can't believe you're going to make me do this," he said. "This is definitely illegal."

"Yeah, well, we're also going to need to find a car," Avian replied. "Can't fit all of us on my bike." He tapped the headlight.

"A car?" Cyn perked up. "I can get us a car."

Avian turned around to glance at her, and the excited look in her eyes was the same one Shelley always had when she used to talk about stealing cars. It was like seeing a ghost. And while that usually didn't do anything for him, this time it made him feel like his head was screwed on wrong.

"We can use his," Avian said with a harsher tone than he intended. He jerked his head at Joe. *"Right?"*

"Uh, yeah. Yeah. It's in the carport. I'll get the keys."

He returned a minute later with the keys and an orange toolbox. They followed him around the side of the house, and Avian didn't miss Cyn's snort of disgust when a battered brown sedan came into view.

"Where do we go now?" Joe asked as they crammed into the front bench seat alongside him.

"The cemetery," Avian replied.

Chapter Thirty-Seven

Cyn grew more and more anxious the closer they got to the cemetery. They were going to pass the house where she and Hunter had lived after high school graduation. *Where Hunter died . . .*

She couldn't look when it finally came into view. And long after it was blocks behind them, she could have *sworn* she still heard police sirens.

Curved wrought-iron gates marked with an elaborate *S* on top of one and an *H* on top of the other greeted them when they pulled up to the sprawling Sleepy Hollow Cemetery. The gates were padlocked shut, but a low stone border with a section of trees and bushes cleared back was obviously used as a way to get around them.

Thirteen led the way into the cemetery, and Cyn and Joe followed. But Cyn kept stopping to look over her shoulder. It felt like someone else was behind them.

Finally, Thirteen stopped and turned around too. "If you're going to keep following us, then you might as well help us. Where did the crossover happen?"

Cyn and Joe both stared into the darkness.

"Who are you talking to?" Cyn said.

Thirteen snapped his fingers, and suddenly her vision blurred and then returned. Everything around her became sharper and more defined. Like she'd been wearing the wrong glasses but now had the right prescription. "I'm talking to *him.*"

He pointed at a mausoleum to their left. Or more accurately, to the young guy leaning against the mausoleum. He had white-blond hair and the greenest eyes Cyn had ever seen.

"Whoa, man," Joe said. "Where did *you* come from?" Then he mumbled, "I don't like ghosts."

"I don't like people who step on graves," the guy said. Joe looked down and saw he was standing on top of a cracked tombstone buried in the ground. Swearing, he took a step back. The guy smirked, then nodded at Cyn. "Hey, Cyn. Abbey will be happy to see you again."

A brief image of black curly hair and blue eyes flashed through Cyn's mind.

"He's one of the Shades that guard the cemetery," Thirteen said to Joe.

Suddenly, a female voice drifted over from the iron-gated plot behind them. "See you tomorrow, Mr. Irving. Caspian? Where are you? I have an idea for this new perfume I want to make, but I need some—"

A girl holding a basket of flowers stepped through the gate and onto the path. She was wearing an old-fashioned lacy black dress and had a red ribbon in her dark, curly hair. Her blue eyes grew huge when she saw them standing there. "Cyn! What are you doing here?"

Dropping the flowers, the girl ran to hug Cyn.

Cyn was almost knocked over by the force of her excitement, but as soon as they touched, memories started flooding back. "Abbey? I don't understand. . . . I have all of these memories of you, but it's like . . . two different things happened. You were alive, and we went to school together. But then everyone thought you were dead. That can't be right."

Abbey pulled back and smiled. Then Caspian came over, wrapping an arm around her waist to pull her closer to him. Abbey tilted her head back to glance up at him. The look that passed between them spoke of a love that was stronger than time.

Cyn had to glance away. It reminded her too much of Hunter.

"Both memories *are* right," Abbey said. "We became friends at school because my best friend, Kristen, died. Vincent Drake was the one responsible for her death." A dark look crossed her face, and she scowled. "The other Revenants helped me cross over and reversed time so that Kristen could come back and I could take her place. On the night that Caspian and I completed each other, Vincent tried to use you to stop me. But it didn't work. Caspian and I ended up together. Here."

"The other Revenants . . . ," Thirteen said. "Let me guess, Acacia and Uriel?"

Caspian nodded. "And Kame and Sophiel. Even Vincent's partner was here, Monty."

"Actually, I think I remember seeing *you* before," Abbey said to Thirteen. "When Cacey and Uri took me with them to go find Monty at the insane asylum, Gray's Folly. I remember thinking it was strange because you were acting like you worked there, but you wore black leather pants."

Caspian raised an eyebrow at her. "You noticed his *pants*?"

"Well, he's . . . uh, he's wearing them now." She gave him a weak smile. "So it sort of just jogged my memory. And you have to admit, it's pretty weird for a nurse's aide to be wearing leather pants."

"I was looking for a psychic who was supposed to be there," Thirteen said.

Caspian bent down to whisper in Abbey's ear, but Cyn could hear what he was saying. "I can get some leather pants."

Abbey blushed and shook her head. "Trust me," she whispered back. "You don't need them."

They shared another look, but Thirteen interrupted them. "So, you're telling me *five* Revenants were here? To take care of one Shade crossover? That's a lot of firepower."

"They were supposed to be taking care of Vincent, too," Caspian replied.

"Yeah, well, they didn't. Because he ended up in her." He pointed over at Cyn.

Abbey inhaled sharply. "How did that happen?"

"Apparently, I'm an Echo," Cyn said. "Which means I'm a conduit for souls of the dead, and it just so happened that he was one of the dead. Lucky me."

"We need to find out exactly where the Shade crossing happened. The last place that Vincent was corporeal," Thirteen said. "So we can remove him."

"It happened at the river," Abbey replied. "We can take you there."

Thirteen stepped to the side. "After you."

Abbey and Caspian led them down the hill and across the grounds, moving with the easy confidence of two people who were familiar with every inch of the cemetery. They walked hand in hand, and Cyn followed behind. But eventually, Abbey started falling back until she and Cyn were walking next to each other.

"Hey, how's Ben?" Cyn asked. "I haven't seen him since graduation."

"He's good. He and Kristen are together now, actually. She opened a bath-and-body shop downtown called Abbey's Hollow. They stop by here a lot. It's nice to still have the chance to see them, you know?" She laughed. "Even if they can't see me."

"You and Caspian just . . . stay here, then?"

"We live here. There's a cottage on the far side of the cemetery. I wish you could see it. It's *amazing*. Right out of a fairy tale."

"Fairy tales were never my thing," Cyn said. "Judging by the looks flying between you and Caspian, though, it's definitely *your* thing."

"It's weird." Abbey paused for a moment. "I almost feel like I was born for this. Born to be the caretaker of this cemetery and to be with Caspian. Did you ever have a feeling that you were just meant to do something?"

Cyn looked down. "No."

"If you ever do get that feeling, grab on to it and don't let go. No matter what anyone says. It's worth it." They walked in silence for a while longer until Abbey said, "So, what's the deal with him?" She gestured over her shoulder at Thirteen. "He's ridiculously good looking, but *wow*. Intense."

"And arrogant and annoying and thinks he's right about everything." Cyn shook her head. "You don't know the half of it. He's not even really all *that* good looking. He's freakishly tall, and he only wears black. And a motorcycle? He drives a motorcycle, by the way. A rusty, old junk bucket. But it's vintage. Supposedly."

"Mmmmhmm ..." Abbey glanced down at the ground, trying to hide her grin. "Sounds like fun."

"I wouldn't exactly call it fun. I'd call it—"

"It happened there," Caspian suddenly said, pointing at the edge of the river.

Cyn came to a stop. She remembered it now. This was the place where Vincent had tried to take her hostage.

Abbey leaned in and gave Cyn a hug. "Come back and see us anytime. Good luck with everything. " She glanced over at Thirteen. "And good luck with *him*, too. Something tells me you're going to need it."

CHAPTER THIRTY-EIGHT

As Abbey and Caspian headed back to the cemetery, Cyn's stomach tightened into knots. It was pitch black, and she could only see a couple of feet in front of her. She started pacing back and forth. *God, I need a cigarette.*

"So, what now?" she said. "Is it going to be like a séance? I've done those before."

Joe sat his orange toolbox on the ground and started digging around in it.

"It's not like a séance," Thirteen said. "But you can sit down. It won't take much longer."

He sat down too, closing his eyes. A look of concentration came over his face, and the burn marks on his arms started rising to the surface. His horns started growing too.

"Hey," Cyn said. She glanced over at Joe. He was pulling out some long-ass needles and a bunch of little glass bottles from the toolbox. A set of white jumper paddles were next. "What are those for? What are you going to do to me?"

Thirteen opened his eyes. They were red. "I'm going to restart the count."

Comprehension suddenly dawned on her. "That means you have to end it first. Right?"

He didn't answer.

"Which means . . . you have to kill me."

"And bring you back," Thirteen said. "That's why I brought Joe. He's an EMT."

Cyn gave him a doubtful look.

"It's the only way."

So I'm going to die. But if I don't do it, I'll end up dying anyway. After the seventh soul has passed through me. Or after Vincent finally succeeds in getting rid of me.

Joe tested the paddles and then nodded at Avian. "All clear. We're good to go."

Thirteen stood up and walked over to Cyn. His hair was loose around his face, and he was dressed in black leather pants and a long black duster. He would have looked like an average biker if it wasn't for the fully grown horns, red eyes, and scars covering his arms. It was only slightly terrifying to look at him as he stood over top of her.

"Ready?"

Cyn closed her eyes. *This is it. You can do it. This is going to work, and everything will be fine. Once Vincent's gone, you'll be back to normal.* Taking a deep breath, she said, "I'm ready."

She opened her eyes again and he leaned over her, both hands outstretched.

"Wait!"

He pulled back. "What's wrong?"

Cyn glanced over at Joe. "Can you give us a minute? We need to speak in private."

Joe let out an aggravated sigh. "Seriously? Do you have any idea how late it is? I have to work tomorrow, and I need to—"

"Joe!" Thirteen growled.

"Fine, fine. I'll be right over here." He moved a couple of feet away and turned his back to them.

Cyn looked up at Thirteen. *He deserves to know what you did to Father Montgomery. And if you don't come out on the other side of this, then at least he can have some peace.*

"I want you to know . . ." Her mouth went dry, and she had to try again. "I want you to know that in case this doesn't work,

I—I really like your wings. They're the most beautiful things I've ever seen." She closed her eyes again and then opened them. "No. That's not—"

Her voice died off, and he leaned closer. "What?" she heard him say.

But it sounded like he was far away, not right beside her. Darkness blurred the edges of her vision sharp and fast, and Cyn realized she was losing herself again. Vincent wanted out, and he wanted out *now*.

I have to tell him. What if I don't get another chance?

Cyn cleared her throat. She was losing sound again. And were her eyes open or closed? It was too dark to tell.

All she knew was that right before Avian pressed his hands to her chest and filled her with a thousand volts of electricity, she finally got the chance to say, "I was the one who killed Father Montgomery, Avian." She didn't know why she called him by the name Father Montgomery had used, but it felt right. "I'm sorry."

CHAPTER THIRTY-NINE

As Avian pressed his hands to Cyn's heart and prepared to shock it into cardiac arrest, she whispered her confession about Father Montgomery. And the demon side of him slipped.

All the hellfires of rage and hatred and pure damnation boiled over and poured straight out of him in a jolt of electricity so strong that it leapt from his hands and seared the flesh from her bones. A blue-white spark arced between them and popped loudly. She convulsed violently beneath him, and he was thrown backward.

Avian flew through the air and landed hard about twenty feet away. His left arm was twisted at an impossible angle, and he could tell right away that it was out of the socket. Sitting up, he used the ground as leverage to push it back in and ignored the screaming pain inside his head.

One bone-crunching sound later, his arm was good as new again.

"Joe," he called. "Is she okay? Is she back yet?"

Joe was bent over Cyn, frantically working on her. He stabbed her with a needle from a bottle marked ATROPINE and then switched to another bottle marked EPINEPHRINE. "It's too much," he yelled back. "It was too much! Too many volts."

He tried the paddles, but they didn't work either, so he started manual compressions on her chest, counting the rhythm out loud and stopping to give her breaths. He did this again and again, but Avian realized that it was taking too long. Too much time had passed.

She wasn't going to make it back.

Joe gave up after the tenth try. His eyes were red, and he rubbed a hand across his face. "You said you had this under control. That this would work. It didn't work! She's fucking dead! Do you realize what you just made me do?" He stared listlessly at the medical supplies littering the ground around them. "What did I do?" he said softly.

Avian didn't notice that his wings had come unbound as he stood up and made his way over to Cyn. He *knew* that she didn't kill Father Montgomery. Just like he knew she didn't kill Hunter. The damn demon inside him had taken advantage of the fact that she thought she was a murderer, and now he was the one who had to make it right.

Crouching down on one knee, he gathered her limp body and put his ear to her chest. Her lips were blue. A streak of blood dribbled out of her left ear. *Breathe, damn it. Breathe!*

But she was gone.

Placing a hand on Cyn's forehead, he threw out five hundred years of promises to himself and tapped into the *other* side. As much as it was a struggle to hold the demon side at bay, the angel side didn't do him any good, so he'd never had any use for it.

Now it was time to see if it was good for something.

Memories of Cyn and Hunter laughing at an old movie, smiling as they cooked breakfast together, and running through a sprinkler late at night, blasted through him. Then they were lying in the back of an old pickup truck. Looking up at the stars. And when Cyn looked over at him, he almost thought for a minute that she was seeing him instead of Hunter.

He would have given anything to keep that look of happiness on her face.

Then Vincent surfaced. Cyn's face twisted as his features took over hers. A viscous tarlike substance creeped over the edges of the picture, but then it was suddenly pulled back. Vincent's face stretched into a parody of itself, and he silently screamed. The memory started to swirl like it was being sucked down a drain, the last vestiges of black trying to hold on tightly around the edges, clawing for that last little bit that he didn't want to give up, but it didn't work. He was pushed out. Pushed on. And he slowly disappeared.

The memories changed one last time. Flashes of a gardener tending to her rows of plants, an earth witch gathering herbs by the light of a full moon, and a professor teaching his class the intricacies of F. Scott Fitzgerald. They were the souls who had lived through Cyn.

And then Shelley's face came into view. Grinning as she slid behind the wheel of a car she'd just charmed someone out of. Crying while she read a sad book. Contemplating the best way to organize her closet. . . .

The sound of Cyn inhaling deeply pulled Avian back to the present. And when she took a couple of short, jerky breaths and looked up at him with wide green eyes, he knew then that a part of Shelley would always be inside her.

Because Shelley had been one of the souls to pass through her.

CHAPTER FORTY

Avian's phone rang in his jacket pocket while he was still looking down at Cyn, and when he moved to answer it she saw his wings.

They weren't black anymore. They were snowy white.

"What happened?" she asked. But other than giving them a brief glance, he didn't have time to answer. Moving farther away, he took his call.

"Hey, Mint. You got good news for me?" There was a pause, then he said, "Yeah. It worked. We're here now, so I guess we'll see how it goes. Thanks. I owe you one."

All Cyn could do was stare at his wings. In the dark, they were especially vivid. With his horns now gone, and the burn marks covered, Avian looked like one of those fallen angels they liked to plaster all over romance-book covers.

He scowled when he turned back around and caught her staring. "Sorry," Cyn said. But she wasn't really.

Avian took his jacket off and folded his wings in before carefully putting the jacket back on. "Son of a bitch," he muttered. "These are going to stick out."

"Hair dye," Cyn offered. "Black hair dye should work."

"Great. Like I need one more thing on my to-do list."

For some reason, that struck her as absurdly funny, and Cyn laughed at him.

"Is that amusing?" Avian asked.

Cyn grinned. "Actually, I find everything amusing right now. I feel good. *Really* good. I can't believe it actually worked. Vincent's gone!" She stood up and looked around. Everything felt different.

Then she noticed that Joe's orange toolbox and medical supplies were gone. "Hey, where'd Joe go?"

Avian glanced around too. "Guess he took off. Things weren't looking too good at first."

Cyn opened her mouth to ask what happened but then shook her head. "You know what? I don't want to know. It's all good now. And even if I'm not totally fixed, if another soul comes along, at least it's not Vincent."

They started heading back through the cemetery, and Cyn couldn't believe how good she felt. *Happy.* Which was something she hadn't felt in a long time. Not even the realization that if Joe was gone then their ride was gone too could dampen her mood. They could always walk back to pick up Avian's motorcycle.

When the cemetery gates came into view, Cyn finally brought up the car situation. "You know that if Joe's gone, we don't have a ride, right?" she said. "I mean, we can walk. It's no big deal, but I—"

"I don't think that will be a problem," Avian said.

"Why not?"

"Because we can get a ride with him."

Avian pointed beyond the gates, and Cyn looked to see what he was pointing to. A white car was sitting there, with a guy standing by the front of the hood.

The guy took a step toward them, and Cyn's heart stopped for the second time.

"Hunter?"

For a dead guy, Hunter Vasquez looked pretty good.

As she stood staring at him, Cyn wondered if this was all a trick and she was dead too. If she'd never really woken up after Avian stopped her heart.

"Can you see him?" she finally said. "Avian, can you see a guy standing over there? Is he . . . alive? Or dead?"

Avian took a minute to answer. "That's something you should ask him."

Cyn frowned, but Hunter started moving toward her. "Cyn!" he called out. "Cyn!"

"Keep it down!" Cyn started walking to him. "Don't you have any respect for a cemetery?"

Hunter pulled back and waited for her to come the rest of the way. As soon as she got close enough to the car, she could see a bouquet of red roses sitting on the passenger seat. "Either this is the most cliché afterlife dream *ever*, or this shit is really happening," she muttered.

Crossing her arms, she stopped just short of him. "What. The. Fuck. Is. This."

"I know this is confusing, but I—"

"You were dead, Hunter. I *saw* it with my own eyes. I *killed* you!"

Hunter shook his head and held out his hands in a pleading gesture. "I know you think that, and I'm sorry. I never thought it would go this far."

"*What* would go this far? Were you playing some kind of sick frat-boy prank on me?"

Avian came up behind Cyn and stopped beside her. "In case you haven't figured it out yet, you didn't kill your boyfriend."

Cyn whirled around to face him. "Oh, yeah, you think? Did *you* have something to do with this too? Is this all one big joke? Who the hell are you to—"

"I'm the guy who realized you didn't kill him when I read your memories and didn't see it there. The only memory you had was of waking up next to him. So I made a call to a friend in Louisiana, Mint, and he looked into it. He's the one who gave me the dirt on Hunter's brother, by the way."

"So, what, you were, like, working some case or something? Playing detective?" Cyn spat.

"No. I was trying to help someone." Avian moved closer and held her gaze. *"You."*

Looking up at him made Cyn suddenly remember what it was like to be right up against his chest, and the back of her neck grew warm. She readjusted her wig. "What happened, then? Why did I wake up in bed covered in blood?"

Avian looked pointedly over at Hunter.

"There are these . . . people that I know," Hunter said slowly. "Actually, my brother knew them, and he helped me get some work with them."

Cyn's eyebrows shot up. "Oh my God, Hunter. Was it the vamps?"

"You know about them?" Hunter's face was filled with surprise.

"Yeah. Your fucking brother stalked me and then kidnapped me because he thought *I* was the one responsible for your murder." She laughed harshly. "Or so-called murder. He said he was working with some vampires that were going to turn him."

Hunter nodded. "The Navarro coven."

"So, when were you going to tell me about this little surprise?" Cyn asked. "And how does your not being dead play into it?"

"You weren't supposed to be brought into it at all. Those were the rules. I did the job for them, they left you alone. But then Declan mentioned that he wanted to be turned, and somehow they thought I wanted to be turned too." He glanced away. "In order to do that, you drink their blood and then . . . you have to die."

"So that's what happened. One of these little vamp buddies of yours 'killed' you to turn you. And I got stuck picking up the pieces."

"You didn't *exactly* pick up the pieces, Cyn." Hunter's face turned hard. "You just left me there. You stole a car and ran."

"Because I thought you were *dead*!" Cyn exploded. "And I

thought I was the one who went psycho and killed you! Do you have any idea what that was like, Hunter? The hell that you put me through letting me think I was a *murderer*?"

"I didn't think it would turn out like this."

"That's the part that hurts the most." Cyn's voice was sad. "You didn't think about this at all."

She turned away from him. Looking up at Avian again, she searched his eyes. "You really didn't believe I did this, even from the beginning, did you?"

"No. And for the record, you didn't kill Father Montgomery, either. Declan did. The police investigating the murder told me they found his hotel room, and there was evidence in it that points to him going to the church to find you. He must have run into Father Montgomery there and thought he could make him tell him where you were."

"But I had a knife. And I remember finding it there, in the church."

"You found it after the fact. You never actually saw Father Montgomery, you just picked up the knife and left. Probably because of what happened in Sleepy Hollow."

"So Father Montgomery died . . . protecting me?" Cyn's voice broke.

Avian reached down to touch her cheek. The rosary beads

were still tied around his wrist. "He died doing something honorable. He wouldn't have had it any other way."

Cyn briefly turned her face toward his hand. "Thank you," she whispered. She glanced up one more time at him and then pulled away. "Don't come looking for me, Hunter," she paused long enough to say. "*Ever.* No matter how long you live."

Then she turned back to Avian and gave him one last smile before heading toward the exit to the parking lot. "And you? Do me a favor and get a helmet, okay?"

Hampton Falls, NH
Two weeks later

Carefully slipping into Lenny's room at Our Lady of Mercy Hospital, Cyn left the door cracked behind her. Visiting hours were long over, but she had a debt to repay.

Reaching into her pocket, she pulled out a brand-new, unopened packet of cigarettes.

"Here you go, Lenny. Now we're even. And you don't have to keep track of it anymore in that goddamn steel trap of yours."

The memory of him saying that made her smile, and Cyn gently placed her hand on the patch of unburned skin right above his elbow. "I'm sorry as hell this happened to you. But that bastard who did it is dead now. He took a short walk and a long drop off the edge of a cliff. You'll never have to see his face again."

The back of her head itched, and she reached up to scratch it. The wig she was wearing was cheap. But it made her feel better to have it on. Protected.

The tattoo outline of the number thirteen on the back of her neck itched too. It was still fresh.

Placing the cigarettes on the stand next to the bed, she gave Lenny a two-finger salute on her way out the door. "Thanks for always looking out for me, big guy. I hope I get the chance to see you and Marv again."

She didn't see the vintage 1948 Vincent Black Lightning following her as she stole another car and pulled out of the hospital parking lot. Which was just fine with Avian. He had a lot of thinking to do and a lot of open road to do it on.

She headed south. And Avian was willing to bet the Vincent Black Lightning he was on that she was going to the deep south. Back in Sleepy Hollow, he'd mentioned Mint in Louisiana to her, and just last week Mint let him know about a call he'd received from a girl asking if he was hiring.

At least she wasn't running anymore. But just because she wasn't running didn't mean she wouldn't need someone to look out for her.

Good thing Louisiana was nice this time of year.